LOVE MATCH

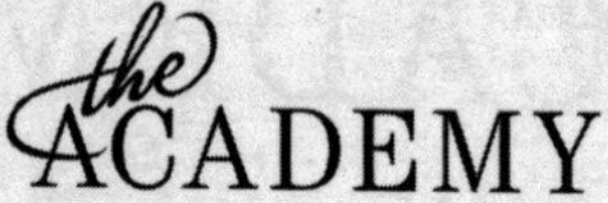

Game On

Love Match

LOVE MATCH

MONICA SELES

AND PAUL RUDITIS

BLOOMSBURY

LONDON NEW DELHI NEW YORK SYDNEY

Bloomsbury Publishing, London, New Delhi, New York and Sydney

First published in Great Britain in February 2014 by Bloomsbury Publishing Plc
50 Bedford Square, London WC1B 3DP

First published in the USA in February 2014 by Bloomsbury Children's Books
1385 Broadway, New York, New York 10018

A CIP catalogue record for this book is available from the British Library

ISBN 978 1 4088 4299 7

Printed and bound in Great Britain by CPI Group (UK) Ltd, Croydon CR0 4YY

1 3 5 7 9 10 8 6 4 2

www.bloomsbury.com

To my father and mother
for letting me dream big
and follow those dreams

Chapter 1

Thump-pop.

Thump-pop.

Thump-pop.

The rhythm was erratic. Most people couldn't dance to the beat. But Maya Hart reveled in the sound. The music filled her body as she moved across the court, striking the ball and sending it back at her opponent. It hit the ground with the deep bass of a *thump* followed by the stringy twang of the *pop* as Donata Zajacova sent it back over the net at her. Maya was exactly where she was supposed to be.

There were occasional breaks in the rhythm when Maya or Donata hit the ball before it struck the ground. A few *pop-pop-pop* volleys brought a staccato intensity to their play. Occasionally silence followed a *thump* until the crowd broke out in a mixture of cheers and groans as the score increased.

This wasn't Maya's first competition. She'd been playing

the junior tennis circuit for years, but this game was different in so many ways.

The Ontario Open was her first international competition. True, the venue was just over the border into Canada, but Maya had never even had a passport until she started at the Academy. Getting that passport was one of the prerequisites for admission to the school.

The Open was also her first tournament since deciding to go pro. Playing with professional status meant she'd be ranked against all the other female tennis players on the circuit. She could now call her idols peers. She could also win some serious bank if she took this all the way.

"OUT!"

Maya glared at the line umpire. He was right, of course. She couldn't challenge the call. But he didn't have to sound so happy about it.

Maya didn't expect anyone on the court or in the crowd to be on her side. She was just some sixteen-year-old nobody playing way out of her league. Donata Zajacova was the star. The phenom had been breaking records since Maya first picked up a racket. But Donata had started getting noticed at sixteen, too.

It still amazed Maya to think she was on the same court as someone she'd been a fan of for years. Never mind the fact that she was holding her own. More than holding her own, actually. She could win this. *Maya* could win this. Sure, she was behind a point, but this was the first time Maya actually believed she had a chance. She'd been too shocked at making it into the semifinal to entertain the thought that she might actually *win*.

Focus, Maya, she warned herself as Donata prepared to serve. It was finally match point. The score had been tied for what felt like forever. If Donata scored, she'd win. Maya had to make sure that didn't happen. Then she needed to score three times to tie it again and then advance. It would be difficult, but not impossible. All she needed was a rally.

Pop.

Thump.

Pop.

Serve. Bounce. Return.

Maya's body ran on instinct. All thought suspended as her reflexes kicked in. Two months of training at the Academy had brought her to a level of play she'd never experienced before. The extra work she'd been putting in on her own strengthened her game.

She'd been completely free of distractions the past two weeks. No drama. No diversions. No guys. If she could hold on, she'd advance to the finals.

She'd take on Nicole King.

Thump-pop.

Thump-pop.

Thump-pop.

Whiff.

Thump.

Inches. Maya swung her racket and missed by inches. The ball hit the ground and bounced toward the back wall.

"In!"

Maya's knees nearly gave out. The energy drained from her body.

She lost. She'd come so close. But that was it. The tournament was over for her. Time to pack up and go back to the Academy, where she'd start her training over again.

Maya walked to the net to meet Donata. The court seemed much longer than it had during the match. Her legs were heavier now than when she was running all over the clay.

For the first time in the tournament, Maya felt totally alone. No one had come to see her play. Her parents couldn't afford the airfare, hotel, and tournament tickets. Her friends couldn't make the trip. The only person in the stadium who even knew her was Nicole. Having her there to witness Maya's failure was even worse than enduring it by herself.

Maya had to put all that aside. People were taking pictures. She needed to smile. It had to be genuine. The last thing she wanted was a shot of her with a scowl on her face going viral. It was time to suck it up and be gracious in defeat.

She reached a hand over the net to Donata. "Congra—"

"Congratulations!" Donata yelled over the cheers and over Maya. "That was a great game! You really gave me a run for it there."

"Um . . . thanks?"

"We certainly gave them a show!"

"We did?" Maya wasn't used to this "we" stuff. Most of her tournaments ended with a quick handshake, then the victor smiled for the crowd while the loser skulked off in defeat. Donata refused to let go of Maya's hands as they posed together for the cameras with the net between them.

"Look at the clock," Donata said over the crowd that was still cheering.

Maya glanced at the scoreboard and did a double take. Their game had lasted almost four hours. *Four hours!* No wonder her legs felt like concrete.

Maya knew they'd been running long when she checked the clock between sets, but four hours was an incredible marathon of a women's match. Now Maya understood why Donata wouldn't let her leave. They *had* put on a show.

Once the cheers started to die down, VIPs in expensive suits descended on the court. Donata held on to Maya's hand even tighter, pulling her toward the exit.

"Time to go," Donata said.

"But I think they want—"

Donata shook her head, cutting Maya off. "Always leave 'em wanting more!"

Donata raised a hand to wave to the crowd as they walked off the court. Maya did the same, even though she wanted to stay and bask in the applause. People were calling out her name. People *knew* her name! Why would anyone ever leave that?

Pausing at the exit, Donata turned to face the crowd one last time. Maya did the same. The tennis star must have seen the disappointment in Maya's eyes as they both smiled and waved. "Don't worry," Donata said. "It's not over. There's still the press conference."

Press conference?

Maya was so glad she'd listened to Renee. She'd spent so much of her time over the past two weeks preparing her game for the Open that she hadn't thought for a second about her look. Thankfully her friend had that covered.

"Hope you don't mind. I picked up a few things from the pro shop."

That's what Renee had said as she breezed into Watson 26, Maya's dorm room, the day before she left for the tournament. "Few things" was the biggest understatement Maya had ever heard in her life.

Renee had been loaded down with plastic bags with the Academy pro shop logo emblazoned on them. The bags were filled with outfits for every day of the competition—as well as things to wear off the court—all charged to Renee's parents' credit cards.

Maya had fought her, of course. At the time, she never imagined she'd be playing through most of the tournament. She also didn't like other people spending money on her. It only reminded her that she didn't have the money to spend on herself. But Renee had insisted and she was difficult to fight when it came to fashion.

"You're stepping onto the world stage," Renee had said. *"You can't debut in some ratty old tennis skirt that was clearly bought before your last growth spurt."*

Walking into the small reception room of the tennis club with rows of reporters watching her every step, Maya was glad she wore a brand-new, perfectly fitted, robin's egg–blue polo shirt with cream linen Bermuda shorts. It was the right combination of casual and sporty for the event.

Maya had never been in a press conference before, but she wasn't too nervous about it. Donata had won the match. The reporters would probably save all the questions for her. They'd just humor Maya for a few minutes before the tournament publicist announced that time was up and the real show was about to begin.

Maya searched the room to see if anyone was looking at her like they wanted to know her story. It would be totally embarrassing if she sat up there in silence for her allotted time because no one cared about her.

The reporters had their heads down, texting or talking on their phones. They seemed blasé about the whole thing. They'd probably been through dozens of these. Hundreds. Press conferences happen at every professional tournament. It gave the media some sound bites to fill out their stories. Nothing Maya said was going to be on TV. Not even on the Sports News Channel. The Ontario Open wasn't a big enough event. No matter how big it was for Maya.

The reporters' heads rose in unison as the publicist tapped her microphone and brought the room to order, opening the floor to questions. Maya was thrilled to see almost every hand rise. They weren't straining to get out of their seats, tumbling over one another to get a word out, but there was at least some interest in her.

A woman who introduced herself as a writer for the Sports News Channel website got the first question. "Maya, your match today was the longest women's match in the history of the Ontario Open—"

"It was?" Maya blurted out. She knew it had been a long game, but that was news. At least to her.

The SNC writer smiled. "It was," she confirmed. "It beat the Mendal/Kunich match by five minutes. Did you think you had that in you to play at that level of intensity?"

"Ask me tomorrow," Maya said, wondering herself how much her body was going to ache the next day. It caught her off guard when the reporters laughed at her comment. She'd made a joke! And they laughed!

"But seriously," Maya quickly added. "I've been training for this for years. Just like everyone else here. We've all spent endless hours on the court. So in that way, I kind of hope I'd be prepared. On the other hand, I don't think anything can prepare you for this level of competition. And to play a match against one of my idols—*Donata Zajacova*—who could *ever* be prepared for something like that?"

The hands rose again. Everyone in the room had a question for Maya. Well, everyone but a grumpy-looking reporter in the front row. He was clearly listening, but he didn't seem all that engaged.

The publicist called on a guy in the back of the room.

"What's your takeaway from the tournament?" the reporter asked. "How was it playing against your idol?"

"I'm mostly glad I didn't go home the first day," Maya said. "Having the chance to play against Donata is more than I could have asked to get out of this tournament. She's such a powerful competitor. I learned more on that court today than in any training session in my life."

The conference continued, with Maya getting more and more comfortable with each question. At one point, Maya stopped being nervous and started talking like she was with friends. She could see herself doing this more often. A lot more often.

Maya never forgot where she was, of course. She wasn't

with friends. She was in a room full of reporters who liked to make stories out of nothing. She was careful to keep her comments focused on the game and praising her opponent. Maya even managed not to cringe visibly when Nicole King's name came up.

All in all, the press conference wasn't nearly as horrible as she'd been dreading. In fact, it was kind of fun. By the time the publicist wrapped things up, Maya was surprised to see that they'd run over by five minutes. And people still had questions for her.

Maya gave an apologetic smile, thanked the reporters, and threw them a wave as she was escorted to the exit at the back of the room. Before she even reached the door, she heard cameras clicking over Donata's entrance from the front. With all heads turned that way, Maya decided to hang back and watch a bit. It probably wasn't appropriate, but she didn't care. She wanted to hear what Donata had to say.

This time, no one waited to be called to order as the reporters started throwing out questions before Donata even sat in the chair that Maya had just vacated.

"Now, now," she said. "There's enough of me to go around. One at a time, please." Donata gave them a sly smile and called on the gruff-looking reporter in the front row who hadn't been interested in asking Maya any questions.

"Donata," the reporter said, "your performance so far in this tournament has been your best since your win at the Australian Open over a year ago. Do you think today's victory will stop some of those articles about you being past your prime?"

The rudeness level of that question shocked Maya. It was

bad enough that people had been writing that about Donata before the match, but to actually call it out to her face was tactless. Maya wasn't the only one to notice as people shifted uncomfortably in their seats.

Donata's laugh broke the growing tension in the room. "Oh, Maxie! I think you're in a better position to answer that question. Will my performance today stop *you* from writing those articles?" Her infectious smile had everyone in the room laughing along with her, including the obnoxious reporter, Maxie.

"And before you all decide that my showing today was because I had a weak opponent, let me stop you right there." Donata looked to the back of the room, flashing Maya a warm smile before turning her attention back to the press. "Maya Hart is one of the most intense players I've gone up against since I first set foot on a court. She has a slice serve that draws you out to the doubles lines like I have never seen before. When you start up those boring stories again about my potential 'successor,' you be sure to include this girl's name on your lists."

It was an incredible endorsement. Reporters had been writing those "boring stories" about "the next Donata Zajacova" for years, but this was the first time the world-famous pro had actually commented on any of it.

Maya wanted to run up to the front to thank Donata. She didn't care if it stopped the press conference. It was the single best thing anyone had ever said about her ever. Maya must have looked like she was about a half second from making that run up to the dais, because the publicist's assistant politely, yet firmly, pulled her out of the room with an offer of something almost as exciting as Donata's endorsement.

Maya had to force herself to stop replaying the press conference over in her mind. She'd drive herself crazy second-guessing her answers and wondering what else Donata might be saying about her right at that moment. There was no point going over it all, since nothing could be done about it now. Instead, she focused on more important things, like calling her parents.

The publicity assistant had been kind enough to let Maya use the phone in his boss's office. Maya had wanted to stick around to talk to Donata after the press conference, but she was told that the tennis star had to rush to some one-on-one interviews. The trade-off was that Maya finally had the chance to call home.

Not having an international calling plan on her cell phone meant that Maya hadn't been able to speak with any friends or family since she arrived for the tournament. Toronto was about a thousand miles closer to Syracuse than she was when she was at school in Florida, but she couldn't afford to make a simple call home because of the invisible line separating the United States from Canada.

None of that mattered now that she had an actual phone tied to someone else's bill. She dialed the familiar number that she'd learned in kindergarten. It was one of the few numbers she had memorized without having to look it up on her phone.

"Maya!" her mom's voice yelled as soon as she picked up.

Maya looked down at the unfamiliar phone on the desk. "Mom? How did you know it was me?"

"How many other people would be calling from a Canadian area code?"

"Oh, yeah. Right." Maya gave herself a mental slap in the head. "Guess what?"

"You and Donata Zajacova had the longest women's match in the history of the Ontario Open!"

Maya looked down at the phone again. Caller ID couldn't possibly have told her all that.

"I've been following the tournament online," her mom explained. "You made the front page of the Sports News Channel website. Well, only Donata's mentioned on the front page, but you're in the article that follows after the jump."

Maya hadn't even had a chance to see what people were writing about her. Like the surprise press conference, Maya hadn't actually thought anyone *would* be writing about her.

Maya's mom relayed the highlights of the articles she'd read so far. It was only basic information on the game, since the reporters and bloggers from the press conference hadn't started to post their stories yet. Even before Donata complimented Maya, people had already been touting her as "the Next Big Thing."

After ten minutes of catching up, Maya heard her father's voice in the background trying to interrupt. Her mom reluctantly said her good-bye and handed over the phone.

"Hey there, Ace!"

"Dad!" Maya practically yelled into the phone. "You would have loved it. Donata Zajacova knows my name!"

"Of course she does," he replied. "Pretty soon everyone will."

Maya's dad was even prouder than her mom, if that was possible. She'd really won the prize when it came to supportive parents. Maya suspected that there weren't many others who would let their teenage daughter move to another state to pursue her dream and travel the globe with only minimal adult supervision.

"Tell me all about the tournament from the start," her dad said. "You are calling on a tennis club phone, right?"

"Yes," Maya said. "We've got hours."

Maya would never let the call go that long. She already felt guilty for using the phone at all, but that couldn't compete with the excitement of sharing this moment with her parents. No other loss in her lifetime had felt like such a win.

As the conversation continued, Maya began to notice that her father's voice sounded strained. He did his best to cover it up, but Maya had heard it before. "Dad," she said tentatively, "did you hurt your back again?"

There was a pause. "It's nothing, Maya."

Suddenly she hated being so far from home. She could imagine him laid out on the couch while her mom did everything around the house without any help. "How bad?" she asked.

"Not like last time," he said. "I just sometimes forget I can't lift those bags of grass like I used to. So tell me, what's the prize for making it to the semifinal?"

Maya wasn't ready to change the subject, but she knew her father was done talking about it. "Enough money that I can actually pay you back for the tournament fees, plane ticket, hotel room, and everything else I've put on the emergency credit card since I signed up for this thing. And maybe have enough left over to buy a meal on the plane home."

"Oh," he said. The word only had two letters in it, but it was filled with disappointment. Not in Maya, naturally, but . . . something. Maybe he hadn't changed the conversation. With his back hurting, he'd have to subcontract lawn-mowing jobs out to his friends and competitors. Money would be even tighter than usual. The little amount that Maya would clear after taxes for being in this tournament wasn't nearly enough to help out.

"Only the winner gets the big cash prize," Maya said, answering the unspoken question.

"At least tell me you get an ugly trophy to go with the other horrible awards in your bedroom here," her dad said. They had a running joke about the tacky trophies she'd collected throughout her junior career. "You really need to start decorating that dorm room of yours."

"Sorry to disappoint you, but no."

"Maybe we should ship some down to you," he suggested. "I'm sure your friends would love to see the Syracuse Tennis Star trophy."

"Don't you dare!" she shouted into the phone. It was the tackiest award ever created: a tennis ball with eyes and a mouth glued on it was mounted on a pair of copper legs with copper arms holding a tennis racket. It was supposed to look like a cute animated character, but the way the eyes were slightly skewed made it more demonic than adorable. For years, Maya and her dad had been trading it back and forth—hiding it in each other's bedrooms, leaving a little nightmarish surprise for the other to find.

"No, no, no," he said. "I know how much you must miss it. I'll be sure to ship it ground so it takes a while to get there."

"Maybe they'll even lose it in transit," Maya joked.

"We can hope."

The two of them laughed some more before Maya finally said good-bye and hung up the phone. She tried not to worry too much about the money situation, since her scholarship covered school and incidentals, but it was hard not to be concerned standing there in the clothes her friend had bought for her. Like it or not, image was an important part of the sports world. And image didn't come cheap.

Chapter 2

It killed Maya to be watching the match between Donata Zajacova and Nicole King. Sitting in the stands was for the spectators, not the players. She wanted to be on that court. If only she hadn't blown her chance the day before.

No matter how many people congratulated Maya on her stellar performance, it didn't change the facts. She hadn't advanced to the final. She was a spectator like everyone else.

But she and everyone else were getting one heck of a game.

Donata ran Nicole all over the court. Honestly, they were both all over the place, but Maya liked to think that Donata had the upper hand. It made for a better story if Maya managed to fight off the eventual winner of the tournament for almost four hours. And watching Nicole go down hard would make Maya's own loss sting a bit less.

Maya still wasn't sure what she'd done to get on Nicole's

bad side. Or if Nicole even had a good side. Sure, Maya had dinged Nicole's new car shortly after showing up at the top-level sports academy. But Nicole had just waved that off like it was nothing.

Did she feel threatened? Maya hadn't done anything that could possibly concern a player at Nicole's rank. Not back then, at least. Now Maya worried that her performance at the Open just put a bigger target on her back.

As much as Maya wanted to be in the final, that probably would have sent Nicole over the edge. Maya wouldn't have stood a chance against her yet. She needed more training. But they'd have their day in the future. Maya and most—but not all—of the press were already looking forward to it. News articles coming out of the tournament were already calling Maya "someone to watch," using words like "impressive" and "powerful" and her personal favorite phrase, "future phenom."

Donata was pretty phenomenal herself in the final, while Maya still ached from their game a day earlier. That was nothing new. Playing through pain was all part of the life. But playing with Donata's skill was something Maya only imagined before she got to the Academy. Now it was expected of her. At times it was exciting, but more often it was terrifying.

"Nicole's not looking that good, is she?" a male voice said behind Maya, pulling her from her thoughts. The owner of the voice was insane. Much as Maya hated to admit it, Nicole was playing a perfect game.

"No," a woman's voice agreed. "This match should have been over by now. Nicole was much better in Prague."

"That was a match," the man agreed.

Maya knew the tournament they were talking about. She'd seen clips online. Nicole looked as good here as she did there. Better, even.

"And of course," the man said, "Donata hasn't looked good since her win at the US Open in—when was that?"

"Two years—"

"Two years ago," he agreed, completely ignoring the fact that Donata had won the Australian Open since then. "Frankly, if Nicole can't finish off someone whose career is on the decline, maybe she's not worth the press she's been getting."

Maya wanted to turn around and give them an impromptu lesson about tennis. They didn't have a clue what they were saying. But she didn't want to draw any attention to herself, and she certainly didn't want to do it by defending Nicole King.

"Then again," the woman said, "maybe Donata's making a comeback. That girl she played against yesterday did look pretty good. What was her name?"

Maya's ears perked up even more. They were talking about her. And it didn't sound negative.

"That Maya girl? Yeah. She could be one to watch."

Now Maya really wanted to see who was talking about her, but she couldn't. It would be awkward and embarrassing. They'd see the huge smile spreading across her face and think she was a total egomaniac. She kept her eyes forward and focused on the court.

The game play was intense, right up to the final point that

came when Nicole smashed an overhead shot right down the baseline.

The stands exploded in a burst of cheers. Even Maya had to clap begrudgingly. Nicole had earned the applause. It was only right to join in. Besides, Maya didn't want anyone seeing her sitting there in silence. That would really give the people behind her something to talk about.

The crowd outside the women's locker room was ten deep. Everyone wanted a piece of Nicole and Donata. The tennis club's publicist and her staff desperately tried to herd the reporters into the press conference, but no one wanted to go.

Nicole's reputation for off-the-cuff comments made this prime stalking area for a good quote about the game. Once she was settled into the press conference with her handlers around, she'd be less likely to blurt out one of her choice comments.

A familiar, clipped British accent rose above most voices in the hall. Nicole's agent, Jordan Cromwell, was on crowd control, but she wasn't pushing the reporters anywhere. She entertained her own court of press, firing off sound bites about Nicole's game. The comments were, oddly, more defensive than celebratory.

"Nicole hasn't had the chance to get much practice in with her packed schedule lately," Jordan said. "We were planning on skipping Toronto entirely, but you all know how she hates to disappoint the fans."

Maya was beginning to think she'd seen a different game

than everyone else in the stadium. Why was everyone acting like Nicole didn't have one of the best games of her life? Was it that much of a surprise that Donata Zajacova was still a strong player?

Maya glanced at her watch. She had to board the airport shuttle soon if she wanted to make it back to school on time. This was her last chance to catch Donata. If only she could get into the locker room.

The tennis club's publicist and Nicole's agent were so busy with the press that they didn't notice Maya pushing her way through the crowd. That left the two security guards stationed at the door. She was prepared to tell them she'd forgotten something and beg them to let her slip in, but they both recognized her from the day before. The door was opened before she could even begin the lie.

"Thanks," she said as she slipped inside.

Even empty, the women's locker room seemed small. It was nothing like the palatial changing rooms at the Academy. All the girls studying tennis could fit in those, along with the guys, the swimmers, and half the football players.

Maya pushed two particular football players from her mind as she went about finding Donata. She'd managed to successfully keep those football players out of her thoughts for most of the tournament. No reason to start now.

It wouldn't be too difficult to locate Donata in the small room. The main problem was avoiding Nicole.

SLAM!

Problem solved.

The slam came from two rows ahead. Even though it made

more sense that the loser of the match would be slamming lockers, that didn't seem Donata's style. That was a Nicole King signature slam.

Maya cautiously stepped into the first row between the lockers, careful not to make a sound in case she'd been wrong about Nicole's location.

She wasn't. Donata had the whole row to herself. She'd finished changing for the press conference and was sitting silently on the bench in a linen pantsuit. She was probably preparing herself mentally to deal with the media. The reporters were ten times more intense than they'd been following the semifinal match. Maya didn't want to disturb her, but there wasn't time to wait.

"Donata?" Maya barely spoke above a whisper. She also didn't want to alert Nicole that she was there.

The way Donata's face lit up when she saw Maya was more than she ever could have expected. "Maya! I was worried I wouldn't get to see you again."

SLAM!

Maya assumed that slam was meant for her, but Donata shrugged it off as she patted the bench for Maya to come sit beside her. "You really put me through the paces yesterday. Thanks for that. It got me better prepared for today."

As she sat, Maya suspected that comment was intended for Nicole's ears as much as her own. "Donata, I don't think I had anything to do—"

Donata cut her off. "Nonsense. And call me Dona. Everyone does."

"Thank you!"

"No need to thank me," she said. "It's my name. Are you sticking around for the presser?"

Maya checked the time on her cell phone. "I have to get back to school."

"You go to the Academy, right?"

"Yes!" Maya was surprised that Dona knew anything about her. "Did you go there?"

"No," Dona said. "The Academy wasn't what it is now back when I was your age. But I'm on the board of directors. Nails Reed likes to stack the board with people who can bring in donors."

"That's right," Maya said. "I knew that." Big-name celebrities in all sports were part of the school board. Famous faces were useful when it came time for fund-raising.

"Truth be told, I haven't been by the school in a while," Dona admitted. "If you're any indication of the current crop of students, I should swing by more often."

Maya blushed. "Thank you."

"You have to stop doing that," Dona said.

Maya looked down at herself. She wasn't doing anything. "Doing what?"

"You need to learn how to take a compliment," Dona said. "It shouldn't always seem like a surprise."

"Oh." Maya felt her face going red again. She couldn't help it. Getting a compliment from one of the top players in the world was a surprise. It would take some getting used to.

Another top player in the game stuck her head around the corner locker. "Excuse me." Nicole's tone was more filled with anger than courtesy. “I told Jordan and that publicist woman that I did not want to be disturbed.”

Even though Nicole was looking right at Maya, it was Donata who replied, voice full of charm. “Oh, I’m so sorry. Was our private conversation disturbing you? This locker room is rather small, but Maya and I were just catching up. Hope you don’t mind.”

“I do, actually.”

“Well, then I’m sorry again. But you look ready to me. If you’d like to go first, I’ll happily wait until after you’ve spoken with the reporters.”

Maya sucked in her breath waiting for Nicole to explode. Everyone knew the winner went second in postmatch press conferences. That’s just how it was done. But Nicole remained calm as she held up her makeup bag. “I still need to put on my game face.”

Dona was just as cool. “I thought your game face was always on.”

“Oh, it is,” Nicole said. “But every now and then I like to freshen things up a bit. You should try it.”

“Some of us don’t require any freshening up at all,” Dona said.

Maya felt like she was watching a rematch, but instead of tennis balls, they were throwing shade at each other.

“You’re on in five minutes,” Nicole reminded her.

“They won’t start without me.” Dona’s smile did not falter. “I’ll be ready before your time is up.”

Nicole walked away, letting out a huff of annoyance as she

went. The sound of her footsteps tapping on the locker room floor got softer as she put some distance between them.

Dona's smile relaxed a bit as she focused back on Maya. "Of course, the Academy produces all kinds of students."

"I'm pretty sure she was like that before she started there," Maya said. She could easily imagine a five-year-old Nicole ruling the playground, deciding who got to swing on the swings and who did the pushing.

"So, what's next, Maya?" Dona asked. "Will you be at Skyborne Cup?"

"I haven't decided yet," Maya said. The Skyborne Cup—named for the car company that sponsored it—was one of the signature events of the year. It was still a couple months away, but Maya wasn't sure she was ready for competition at that level.

"You should seriously consider it," Dona said. "Everyone's going to be there. And you're part of everyone now, kiddo."

"I'll think about it."

"Better decide soon. The deadline is coming up." Dona checked her watch. "You should slip out the back. The reporters will be getting settled by now, but some stragglers may be sticking around outside. They might try to get you to talk about the final. That's fine with me, if you want, but like I said yesterday—"

"Always leave 'em wanting more," Maya said.

Dona smiled again and hugged her good-bye.

Maya agreed with the advice, but in all honesty, she mainly wanted to avoid answering any more questions. She was tired of being "on." The problem was, her escape route took her right by the bathroom where Nicole was primping.

Maya made her way to the back exit walking as lightly as she could, but her shoes betrayed her by clicking with every step. This was the downside of Renee's fashion advice. She'd be much more comfortable in sneakers than heels—quieter, too.

The water was running in one of the sinks in the bathroom area. Maya carefully peeked in the doorway as she passed, but stopped when she saw Nicole making herself up in the mirror. Her hand shook as she applied mascara. It was so bad that she had to hold on to the wrist of her right hand with her left as she guided the brush onto her eyelashes.

Maya knew what it was like for her body to be weak following an intense match. Her legs were even sorer now than yesterday. But this was different. Something was wrong.

Maya debated saying something to Nicole, but she never got the chance. Nicole caught her looking from the mirror. "Get! Out!"

The temptation to act like a concerned friend passed and Maya left. They weren't friends anymore. In truth, they never had been. Nicole had been manipulating Maya for weeks. But that was over and Maya had learned from the experience. The Academy was tough, but it just made her tougher. This tournament had proven as much. She'd made the right decision in staying at the school.

Maya may not have won the Ontario Open, but people were talking about her like she did. More importantly, they were treating her like she did. Maya didn't need to stick around for the final press conference. She didn't need any additional interviews. She'd done what she'd come to do. She did more than she'd hoped to do, actually. Now it was time to go home.

Funny how the Academy was starting to feel like home.

Chapter 3

The hug went on longer than the one Maya shared with her parents when they saw her off at the bus station when she first left for the Academy. It was beginning to feel almost as long as her semifinal match. Maya had only been gone a week. Cleo was just away for a long weekend. But Renee held on to them like they'd just come back from an extended tour of duty. It was weird, but also kind of nice. Maya never had a friendship like this before.

Renee finally let go, stepping back while smoothing out the wrinkles on her dress. "Don't you two ever leave me again!"

Cleo cracked her neck. She wasn't used to hugs like that either. "It's going to be hard to compete in future tournaments if we never leave school."

"We'll host them all here," Renee said. "We have the space for it."

Renee was right. The six hundred acres of the Academy

grounds contained some of the best sports facilities in the world. Tennis courts made of clay, asphalt, grass, and carpet, an Olympic-size swimming pool, and two golf courses designed by the leading course architects were only the tip of the iceberg. But as much as the school was considered one of the premiere institutions in sports training, Maya doubted the tennis, swim, and golf associations would be willing to relocate all their events there.

"Nails Reed would love that," Maya said. The headmaster constantly worked to enhance the image of his school. Maya had been caught up in his drive for promotion. She'd only been at the school for a few months, but her face was already on the Academy brochures.

"Everyone would come to compete against the two newest shining stars in tennis and golf." Renee dropped onto Cleo's bed. Her nose crinkled as she landed on the thin mattress with the squeaky springs. Renee came from a different life and a different side of campus. She wasn't used to slumming it in Watson Hall like Maya and Cleo. She was getting better at hiding her discomfort in the bare-bones room, though.

"I'm no shining star," Cleo said.

"At least you won your tournament," Maya said.

"You won in the press." Renee opened up her laptop. "That's all that matters. Look at all these stories. I bookmarked them."

Renee handed the computer over to Maya. The top-of-the-line laptop was dressed in a designer sleeve that matched Renee's purple shoes. It was like her computer was just another accessory rather than an expensive piece of technology. Yes, Renee and Maya came from vastly different sides of campus.

Several stories were bookmarked, but Maya didn't need to read any of them. Both the planes she'd taken had Wi-Fi, as well as the airport she stopped in for the brief layover. She'd spent the entire trip reading her own press. She would never admit that to her friends because she didn't want to be obnoxious about it, but all the stories had been very positive.

Maya opened up a particularly effusive blog post and pretended to read it for the first time. "Oh, this is nice."

"But the best part is how they're totally trashing Nicole." Cleo grabbed the computer. The pastel design clashed with her black leather jacket and shredded jeans with the artfully placed gray paint splatters. "Check this out."

Maya took the computer back. It was another article she'd already seen, written by Maxwell Lexington—or *Maxie*, as Dona had called him. It was about Nicole's disappointing struggle to win the final against a player she should have shut out of the game from the start.

Maya didn't feel like celebrating over the article. Aside from the fact that it was mean, it was also just plain wrong. Maya had been there. Nicole played well. She was certainly better than the writer led anyone to believe.

"Was she really that bad?" Renee asked with concern in her voice. Renee and Nicole had been friends and roommates since before Maya came to the Academy. Technically they were still friends even though Renee didn't like all the stuff Nicole had put Maya through.

"No, actually. It was a good game. It's just . . ." Maya was about to say something about Nicole's wrist but decided against it. Gossip was a powerful weapon at the Academy. If Nicole was hiding an injury, there were definitely people who would use that information to their benefit. Maya trusted that Cleo and Renee would keep any secret she told them in confidence, but she didn't want to run the risk. There was enough tension between her and Nicole. She didn't need to add more.

Once it became clear that Maya wasn't going to finish her thought, Renee bounced up off the squeaky springs of Cleo's bed. She reached for the small pink box she'd brought with her.

"I got something to celebrate your homecoming." Renee lifted the lid, unveiling a trio of red velvet cupcakes with fluffy white frosting. "They're Vegan Velvet cupcakes, from that new café by the villas. The healthiest cupcakes outside of California."

"'Healthy cupcakes' is an oxymoron," Cleo said, eyeing the small pastries skeptically.

"Just try it!" Renee prompted.

Cleo sneered at the cupcake as she lifted it out of the box.

Maya was suspicious of them also, but she smiled politely as she took her own. It smelled okay and certainly looked and felt like a cupcake. But she was with Cleo on the idea of healthy cupcakes. What was the point?

Renee had enough enthusiasm for all of them. She raised her cupcake into the air as if she was giving a toast. "To victory," she said. "Whether or not you actually won."

"To victory," Maya and Cleo echoed as they "clinked" their cupcakes together.

Maya pulled at the wrapping and took a small, tentative bite. The burst of flavor on her tongue was immediate and intense. The Vegan Velvet cupcake was disgusting. The dry cake sat in her mouth like a stone. She was too afraid to swallow it and spread the horrifying taste through her body.

Cleo spit her mouthful of cake into a tissue without bothering to hide what she was doing. She'd taken out half the cupcake in one bite and wasn't shy about retching from the taste. "Oh my God, that's awful!"

Cleo shoved the box of tissues in front of Maya. She didn't want to be rude to Renee, but she had to get that taste out of her mouth. Maya took a couple of tissues and deposited the slightly chewed bit of cupcake into them, before smiling shyly at Renee. "Sorry."

Renee shrugged it off, putting down her own cupcake. She hadn't bitten into it yet. "If I'm going to cheat on my diet, I'll wait for a tastier treat."

Cleo finished chugging the energy drink she'd grabbed out of the tiny dorm fridge, then turned her attention to Renee's laptop. "Doesn't look like you saved any of my articles."

Renee blushed. "Well . . ."

"It's okay," Cleo said. "I already saw them."

"Oh, Cleo." Maya had read them, too. Even though Cleo had come in first at the Savannah Junior Golf Invitational, no one had written about her game.

"It's not the first time people have commented on my look," Cleo said. "I get stares all the time in class."

Maya had stared the first time she met Cleo, but mainly because she thought her new roommate had committed a bloody murder. In truth, she'd just been coloring her hair red. That was several weeks and at least three different hair colors ago.

Cleo now rocked purple highlights on one half of her head while the other half was black, spiky hair growing back in. It had been completely shaved when Maya had met her. Combine that with the leather skirt and red tank top Cleo had worn during the Invitational and it gave the bloggers something to blog about.

Cleo typed something into the browser and handed the laptop over to Maya and Renee. "Grant Adams is the worst."

She'd brought up a page titled: "Adams Addresses the Ball." The headline of the top article read: "The Death of the Gentleman's Game." It was one of the stories Maya had read on the trip home. And it was horrible.

Maya closed the computer. She couldn't bring herself to read it again. It was all about how Cleo was disrespecting the sport by refusing to dress "normal." As if a sport known for men wearing awful plaid pants knew anything about normal.

"Honestly, though," Cleo said. "I kind of like it."

"Sports marketing is all about branding these days," Renee agreed. "You could promote yourself as the Death of the Gentleman's Game."

Maya was horrified. "Renee!"

"What?" Renee asked. "As long as they're talking about you, it doesn't matter what they're saying."

Maya doubted that Nicole would agree, considering what was being said about her coming out of the Ontario Open. "Who is Grant Adams, anyway?" Maya asked. "He writes like he swallowed an etiquette guide from the nineteenth century. Is he for real?"

Cleo shrugged. "More or less. He's like the most conservative voice in a conservative game. I always expected he'd hate me. No biggie."

Cleo wasn't fooling Maya. There was no question the girl was strong, but being bullied online sucked no matter who you were.

Renee didn't seem fooled either, because as soon as there was a lull in the conversation, she changed the subject. "Let's hit the Underground."

Maya picked up her history textbook. "I'd love to, but I have a ton of homework to catch up on."

Cleo took the book out of Maya's hand and dropped it on her bed. "Maya, you just got back from a huge tournament."

"It wasn't *that* huge."

"Maya, you just got back from a *midsize* tournament," Cleo said. "Manjarrez will let you slide for a couple days. These articles about the tournament are a 'get out of homework free' card."

"You haven't gone out in weeks," Renee said.

"I've been practicing," she insisted.

"You've been avoiding," Renee insisted right back.

Maya didn't have to ask what her friend was talking about. She knew. And she didn't want to discuss it.

"Look," Cleo said. "This isn't up for discussion. I've still got the taste of Vegan Velvet cupcake in my mouth. It's going to take some real food to get rid of it. Besides, I just won the Junior Invitational. There are some people whose faces I need to rub my victory in. You're not going to deprive me of that, are you?"

Maya was stuck. She had been avoiding places like the Underground for the past few weeks. Basically, she'd stayed away from anyplace she might run into *them*.

But Maya was tired of hanging in her dorm room when she wasn't on the court. She also didn't want to stop Cleo from having the fun she so totally deserved in light of her win. Part of her wanted to watch Cleo as she reveled in that victory.

And part of her hoped she might run into the guys she'd been working so hard to avoid.

Even though it was late on a Sunday night, Maya knew the Underground would be packed. It was the best hangout on campus and nobody ventured off school grounds on the last night of the weekend because of early Monday-morning training sessions.

Everyone was going to be there. Which meant *they* were going to be there. No doubt about it. Maya hadn't worked up the nerve to walk through the front door yet, and her friends were starting to notice.

"How many shoes do you have down there?" Cleo asked. "It's sure taking a long time to tie them."

Maya finally stood. "Sorry. Just want to make sure everything is good and tight."

"Uh-huh," Cleo said, nodding. She wasn't buying it.

Maya couldn't hide behind her training any longer. The Ontario Open was over. Sure, the Skyborne Cup was coming up and there would be another tournament after that. Tennis didn't have an off-season like other sports. But that wasn't the point. She couldn't hide from her life anymore. No matter how much it improved her game.

Maya took a breath and started to cross the small parking lot with Cleo and Renee by her side. "I can do this," she said to no one in particular.

"Of course you can," Renee replied.

Cleo let out a snort of sarcasm. "Yes, I believe you can manage—Look out!"

A car horn blared. Tires screeched. And a cobalt-blue Audi R8 swung into the parking spot Maya was about to cross in front of.

"Hey!" she yelled, jumping back with her friends. It took all her control not to fall back on her butt. Her legs strained as she gave her muscles an even more intense workout than she'd had in the game.

The driver's window went down and a perfectly manicured hand waved backward at them. "Sorry. Wanted to get that spot before anyone else."

Maya didn't recognize the car, but she knew the voice. Nicole's direct flight must have gotten in early.

Nicole liked to celebrate her victories with a major purchase. This was the second car she'd bought in the little time that Maya had known her. She probably had to keep winning tournaments to have any money in her bank account.

Maya wondered how it was possible that she had the time to buy it. She must have preordered the car before the tournament and had it waiting for her when she got off the plane.

"You like?" Nicole stepped out onto the asphalt in a slinky

blue dress that matched the car's paint job. She was way overdressed for the Underground.

"Starting your fleet?" Cleo quipped.

"I traded the Aston in," she said. "It hasn't been running right since it got that ding in the side panel."

Maya rolled her eyes. She used to be embarrassed by that ding, which she had caused. But Nicole was being ridiculous. The barely noticeable flaw was minor cosmetic damage. On the other hand, Maya was glad that Nicole had not decided to sue. She could see the drama queen taking things to that level.

"See you inside," Nicole said with a fake smile before turning on her silver heels and sauntering into the club.

The three girls stood in the parking lot, unsure of whether to let loose with some snark or laugh. They just shook their heads in unison and followed. At least it would be easier for Maya to slip in unnoticed. Nicole always made a grand entrance, especially coming off a win.

Nicole was already surrounded by the time they walked into the Underground. Maya had been right. The place was packed. People were even sitting on the pool tables to make room. Everyone else seemed to be making his or her way over to Nicole to congratulate her.

"Guess nobody here agrees with those articles about her win not being a real victory," Maya suggested.

"Hey, a win is a win," Cleo said. "Especially when you have a chance to buddy up to that winner."

Some girl standing by Nicole shouted, "Maya!" and heads turned her way. Maya didn't recognize the girl, but that didn't matter. Several of Nicole's acolytes peeled off, making their way to Maya.

Hands reached out to high-five her as shouts and cheers of congratulations reached Maya. It felt good. And weird. But mostly, it was uncomfortable since Cleo was standing right next to her and she'd actually won the Invitational.

Maya had no doubt where her sudden fame came from. *Everyone* followed Nicole King news. Maya was just caught up in her orbit. She felt better when some of the golf students pushed their way through the crowd to greet Cleo.

Being the center of attention was unusual for Maya. Which was probably why she was so focused on her friends. Once Cleo was taken care of, Maya noticed that Renee was busy flirting with some random guys. Maya didn't worry too much about her, though. Renee was always the center of attention when guys were around.

Strange hands continued to reach out to Maya and she made sure to connect with each one. She knew how it felt to be ignored when she was one of those hands. But making eye contact was a little too much. Who were these random people who didn't care about her a week ago? What did they want from her now?

As the hands withdrew, Maya took in the rest of the club. She tried very hard to not look like she was searching for someone.

Jake was at a small table in the corner with some girl Maya didn't know. Even sitting, the girl looked tall. Like, basketball player tall. But she could have been into any sport, really. Maya was tall, too. Maybe that was Jake's type.

Maya didn't want to be jealous. She was the one who had called it off between them. The breakup came as a result of Jake's actions, but Maya was the one who had made the decision.

In what was either a huge misunderstanding or, more likely, an evil plot, Jake had slept with Nicole. It came about after a lie Nicole had told him about Maya, but that wasn't the point. He gave up on Maya too easily. That made it easier for her to give up on him.

Easier, but not easy.

At least he wasn't one of the people coming over to congratulate her. He was so into his private conversation that he probably didn't even notice she was there. As much as Maya wanted to believe that Jake was giving her the space she needed, it was far more likely that he was just trying to get lucky.

When Maya saw yet another set of fingers reaching for her out of the corner of her eye, she raised her hand, expecting another congratulatory slap. She didn't actually pay attention until the strong hand gently grasped hers and wouldn't let go.

"Wha— Travis!" Unlike his brother, Travis Reed hadn't hesitated to reach out to her, literally and metaphorically.

"Congrats, Maya," Travis said. "I saw the blogs. You're the talk of the tennis world."

"I didn't even win," she said.

"You won in the court of public opinion," Travis said. "That's all that matters." Then he hugged her. It was the friendly kind of hug, nothing more. But it still made Maya uncomfortable. She wondered if she would have minded if the Reed brother hugging her had been Jake.

"Look, Travis," she said as he released her.

Travis held a hand up to stop her. "That was just a hug," he said. "Between friends. We can be friends, right?"

Maya still wasn't sure how involved Travis had been in Nicole's scheme to get Jake into bed and wind up getting a part in a Hollywood movie out of it. To think there was even a scheme for that kind of thing still made Maya's head reel.

Travis was a good guy. Too good, at times. Or too perfect, was more like it. Maya wanted to give him the benefit of the doubt, but she was still skeptical. At the same time, there was no reason they couldn't at least try to be friends while she figured him out.

Well, maybe there was one.

Maya looked over to the corner of the club again. Jake was gone. It bothered Maya how happy she was to see that the girl was still there.

"Maya?" Travis asked. He'd have to be blind not to notice her looking away like that.

"Sure," she said tentatively. "We can be friends."

"Great!" He put a casual arm around her. "As friends, I think we need a round of drinks to celebrate your not victory."

"Yeah," she said as they headed for the bar. "To my *not* victory."

Travis ordered cocktails for Maya and the girls. The Underground specialized in nonalcoholic concoctions that were just as tasty, but without the hangover aftereffects.

Following a toast to the nonvictory that was tastier than her earlier cupcake toast, Maya pulled Travis into a private conversation. “I’m glad you came over,” she said. “That took some guts knowing how things have been.”

“I wanted to give you time,” he said. “And I hoped that with some distance you’d realize I wasn’t part of Nicole’s plan to break you and Jake up. Not a willing participant, at any rate. I’m sorry I put you in that position and I’m truly sorry that Nicole was able to use me to get to you.”

“I know,” Maya said, even though she still didn’t know for sure. “And thanks. I’m glad you came over to say that. It was . . . brave.”

Travis looked unusually shy. “Well, in the interest of honesty in our friendship, I should admit there is an ulterior motive. I have a message to deliver from Dad.”

It was never a good thing when Nails Reed had a message for her.

“He wants to see you in his office first thing tomorrow,” Travis said. “Didn’t tell me why.”

Of course, the only thing worse than a message from Nails was a request for a face-to-face meeting. Once again, the Academy was beginning to feel like home. Except this time, she was afraid of being grounded.

Chapter 4

At her old school, Maya had only seen the principal when it was time for an assembly. Maybe she ran into the woman once or twice in the halls, but she'd never actually spoken with her. And she'd certainly never been called to the principal's office. Maya had only been at the Academy for a few months and she'd already logged more face time with this principal than she had in all her schools combined since kindergarten.

It probably wasn't right to think of Nails as the principal. He was more of a "headmaster." Whatever the correct terminology, he was the head guy in charge and it was never a good thing to be summoned to his office. On the bright side, she didn't have a security escort this time. That was an improvement.

The door opened and Nails flashed her the smile that used to gleam with an extra CGI sparkle in toothpaste commercials. "Maya!"

"Hi, Mr. Reed," she said as he ushered her into his office. Maya still wasn't quite comfortable in there, no matter how plush the smooth leather chairs were. And they were pretty plush.

"Congratulations on your showing in Toronto," Nails said. "It's impressive to see how much of an impact the Academy has had on your game."

Maya blinked twice. That sounded a lot more like a compliment to himself and his school than it was to her and her accomplishments. "Thanks?"

"Nothing makes me happier than seeing a student making the most of her time with us," Nails added. "To think how far you've come in such a short amount of time, I expect you'll be giving Ms. King a run for her money soon enough."

"I'm just here to play," Maya said. She didn't want to give him any ammunition to use against her by letting on that she had issues with Nicole.

Nails nodded. "Yes, that's how we all start out. Only thinking about the game. But I'm sure you've come to see by now how much work it takes to play these games."

Maya honestly had no clue what he was talking about.

"Just look at my son. He puts in more effort than the average student. Not because he's my son. Because he knows that's what it takes to succeed."

Maya didn't have to ask which son he was talking about. Nails rarely brought up Jake as an example, unless it was a bad example. That was one of the things that drew her to Jake in the first place. Maya felt like she was the only one who saw him for who he really was instead of the guy his father made him out to be.

Nails still had to drive his point home. "Travis is there for the school every time I ask. Heck, he's there before I ask: leading tours for prospective students; mentoring younger classmates; standing in for me at events when I'm unavailable."

Maya nodded along with the list of Travis's accomplishments. She already knew most of it. Travis worked his butt off. There was no doubt that he did it to make himself a better student athlete all around, but Nails was fooling himself if he didn't realize Travis did it mainly to please his father.

"With those things in mind," Nails continued, "your school needs a favor."

Finally, he'd come to the point. It must be a doozy of a favor, considering all the lead-up. Did he want her family to make some kind of donation? He knew better than anyone that she was at the Academy on a scholarship.

"We have a new student," Nails said. "Someone you've already met. Diego?"

Maya had almost forgotten all about Diego and the whirlwind trip to Rio with Travis. So much had happened between then and now. It was weeks after Diego said he'd be ready to start at the school. But what could Nails want from her? Diego played soccer. Did he want her to give him a school tour?

"I'm hosting a small reception to welcome him tomorrow night," Nails continued. "Just a few faculty members, the soccer coaches, nothing major. I was hoping to have a familiar face there for him. Would you be free to join us?"

That was it? That was what he'd called her to his office for? To invite her to a party? "Sure," she said.

Nails's mouth opened, but nothing came out. A brief look of surprise crossed his face before he regained his composure. He was smart enough to realize that Maya caught the expression and it now hung between them like an unanswered question. "I'm sorry," he said. "I'm accustomed to negotiating these kinds of things with the students. With Nicole it usually takes several rounds of offers and counteroffers before she agrees to help the school. I don't often get a yes on the first try from anyone who is not my son."

"It sounds like fun," Maya said. Actually, a stuffy reception with the faculty sounded like the exact opposite of fun, but she looked forward to seeing Diego. It wasn't that long ago since she was new at the Academy. She still remembered how overwhelmed she'd felt. It would have been nice to see a familiar face when she arrived.

She also would have liked a small reception in her honor, if she was being completely honest.

"Kicked out again?" Cleo sat curled up in a ball on the edge of the fountain outside of the Administration building. Her eyes remained focused on the screen of her phone as Maya stood over her.

"You can't get a single that easily," Maya replied. "You're stuck with me, roomie."

Cleo finally looked up. "So what was it about? Did he bring you in for a meaningful conversation about his sons?"

Maya let that one go. "He invited me to a party."

"No. Seriously." Cleo read the look on Maya's face. "Seriously? He wants you to go to a party? He couldn't just text you?"

"I guess he wanted to make me feel obligated to go before he asked."

"That sounds like a Reed."

Maya filled Cleo in on the invitation as they walked to class.

"Sounds boring," Cleo said.

"Yeah, but if the biggest favor the school is going to ask for is for me to attend a party—"

Cleo stopped on the walkway so suddenly that she nearly took out a skateboarder who'd been maneuvering to slip around them. "What makes you think that's the only favor he's going to ask for? Maya, you're not even anybody yet and Nails wants stuff from you. I hate to say this, but imagine what it's going to be like when you're at Nicole's level."

"But you're already at Nicole's level," Maya reminded her. "You actually won your tournament."

"A junior tournament," Cleo reminded her right back. "It's not about wins and losses. It's about being the whole package. Look at you! You're the package. I'm just . . . me."

"Cleo—"

"Don't get me wrong," Cleo quickly added. "I like my particular package. But the school won't be trotting me out for any photo ops. Not the Wicked Witch of the Green."

"Don't say that about yourself!"

"I didn't. Grant Adams did." Cleo handed her phone to Maya. That stupid blog was up on the screen. The headline of the latest post was the exact line that Cleo just quoted. The article went downhill from there.

Maya shut off the phone, as if making the blog disappear from the screen would take it off the Internet. "What has that guy got against you?"

"Probably broke his heart to find out I was into girls and would never give him the time of day."

"Cleo, I'm into guys and I'd never give that jerk a second glance. He's probably some loser who lives in his mother's basement watching the Golf Channel all day."

"I was thinking he's locked away in the attic," Cleo said. "Where he's forced to be quiet when his parents have friends over so nobody knows he exists."

"No, they keep him in the doghouse, where—"

"Maya?"

Maya was horrified to think someone had overheard their conversation. She was even more horrified to turn and see that it was Nicole's agent.

"Jordan?" Great. Nicole must have complained about Maya slipping into the locker room after the final. Jordan was probably there to tell her to stay away from her client.

"Isn't this fortuitous, running into you here?" The pleasant tone of Jordan's voice didn't sound like there was a warning on the horizon, but Maya kept her guard up. Cleo, meanwhile, had totally frozen in place unable to speak. Her eyes bugged out like she was excited to be in the presence of royalty.

"Are you looking for Nicole?" Maya asked. It seemed unlikely since Nicole didn't have any morning classes. Jordan, of all people, would know something like that.

"No," Jordan said. "Nicole isn't my only client on campus, you know."

Maya hadn't known that, actually, but it made sense. An agent as powerful as Jordan must have clients all over the world.

"I'm sorry we didn't have a chance to chat at the Open this weekend," Jordan continued. "You played very well."

"Thank you."

"It got me thinking, actually," Jordan said. "I'm always on the hunt for new talent. Call me sometime if you want to talk." A business card appeared in Jordan's hand, almost like magic. Just as suddenly, the card found its way into Maya's palm.

"Chat later?" Jordan said in lieu of good-bye.

Maya watched her walk off, as speechless as Cleo.

"What was that?" Maya finally asked when she found her voice.

"Oh, nothing much," Cleo said. "Just one of the top agents in the business wants you to be her client!" She punctuated her statement by slapping Maya on the arm.

"Ow!" Maya rubbed the spot that was already turning pink. The golfer obviously didn't know her own strength. "Oh, come on. She was just being nice."

"Maya, I've never met her, but Jordan Cromwell doesn't exactly have a reputation for nice. More like for being a barracuda."

Maya slipped the card into her purse. "She probably gives these cards out all the time. If she was really interested in me, she would have set up an appointment or something. She just ran into me."

“You’re kidding, right?” Cleo asked. “Oh, wait. I forgot. You’re still new.”

Maya had been at the school for a couple months, but Cleo was right. Most of the time Maya felt like she’d just stepped off the bus.

“Let me break it down for you,” Cleo said. “Jordan comes to the tennis courts. She’s on the fields, the pools, even stops by the greens from time to time. Occasionally you might see her in the Admin building. But I have never, ever caught of glimpse of her by the classroom buildings. Nails likes to keep the academics away from the business side of things. Most agents don’t care about that, so you see them all over the place. But Jordan Cromwell respects the system. That’s why she gets the first call about students to watch for. She doesn’t want to mess that up by crossing the line.”

“You think Nails called her about me?”

“You really think she needed a call? You’re the story out of Toronto, not Nicole. I can’t say what’s going on behind the scenes, but I do know one thing: running into Jordan here was no accident.”

Maya pulled Jordan’s business card back out of her purse. It was just a small piece of white card stock with some writing on it and a company logo. Nothing special. And yet, suddenly, Maya felt like she was holding on to a golden ticket.

Chapter 5

It was shaping up to be a week's worth of British entertainment for Maya. On Monday she'd gotten a golden ticket. By Tuesday evening she felt like she'd been transported into an old-time English drama.

The Reed mansion was far more contemporary than a British estate, but to Maya, who grew up in a cramped two-bedroom house, it was as big as a castle. But that wasn't the reason she felt like they'd all been transported back in time.

To make Diego feel welcome, Nails had suggested his guests greet the new student when the car they'd sent for him pulled up to the house. Maya was stuck shivering in the chilly night air along with some of her teachers and people she'd never met before waiting for the car to arrive. Surrounded by faculty and coaches, she was probably the only one who felt like part of the serving staff.

Jake was nowhere to be seen, which was likely Nails's

doing. He would never straight-up tell his son that he wasn't invited. That's not the way Nails operated. He would just talk about the party around Jake until it became obvious that he wasn't getting an invitation. Then Jake would do the rest by making himself scarce.

Maya didn't like that she knew so much about the inner workings of the Reed family, but in this case she didn't really mind the result. She wasn't ready to deal with both Reed brothers in such a public setting.

Travis not being at the party was the real surprise. It was exactly the kind of thing Nails liked his favored son to be involved in. Maya wasn't exactly excited about seeing Travis, but they were trying to be friends. She could use a friend right now. Making small talk with adults she barely knew was not a skill she possessed.

After what felt like an eternity, but was probably less than five minutes, a limousine pulled up the long driveway. It was a far cry from the bus that dropped Maya off outside the Academy and probably total overkill for Diego. His life was less privileged than hers. Arriving in a limousine to a mansion with a group of semi-formally dressed people would have intimidated the heck out of her.

The limo stopped at the foot of the stairs and the driver got out and double-timed it to the rear passenger door. He opened the door with a flourish and for a moment Maya felt like she should applaud. She wasn't the only one leaning forward waiting for Diego to make his grand entrance. It all felt so forced. And pointless, considering no one got out of the car.

Maya wondered if Diego had slipped out of the limo on the ride up the nearly endless driveway. He might have taken one look at what was waiting for him and ditched. Maya wouldn't have blamed him. But the driver surely would have noticed. He wouldn't continue to stand there, awkwardly, holding on to the door.

Seconds stretched into minutes with no sign of Diego. The receiving line outside the Reed estate wasn't exactly welcoming, but the Diego she'd met down in Rio didn't seem the type to be easily intimidated. He couldn't possibly be afraid to come out, could he?

Finally she saw some movement inside the car. Everyone else must have seen it, too. The shuffling feet stopped and they all turned their attention back to the car.

Travis's head popped out the door, solving that particular mystery. Of course he'd gone to pick up Diego at the airport. The welcome carpet was probably rolled all the way across the city.

Travis held up the "one moment" finger to his father before disappearing back into the darkened interior. Nails remained stone-faced, as if he was used to this kind of thing.

Maya considered suggesting that they should all wait inside, but she was too afraid to speak up. This group intimidated her, and they weren't even looking in her direction.

Scratch that. One set of eyes had fallen on her: Nails's. She could only assume it was his way of asking for help. Maya wasn't sure what she could do, but she reluctantly stepped forward and made her way to the limo.

Now Maya had all eyes on her. If this was anything like what Diego felt inside the limo, she didn't blame him for staying in there. It was uncomfortable to the max.

"Hello?" she tentatively asked as she peeked in the door.

She was unprepared for what she saw inside. Instead of a frustrated Travis trying to coax a reluctant Diego out of the limo, she found them both playing a video game on the small TV in the back. Diego seemed completely unaware that anyone was waiting for him, but Travis's eyes pleaded with Maya to do something.

"Mind if I come in?" she asked.

Diego's eyes darted to her for a split second. "Maya! Get in here. Grab that controller. Travis sucks at this game."

Maya slipped into the car and took the controller from Travis. The back of the limo was roomy enough that they could probably host the party in there. They had games, music, and even a minibar. It was far more comfortable than the Reed estate.

Maya took control of Travis's robot character. She didn't recognize the game and had no clue what she was supposed to do. "You do know people are waiting, right?"

"Yep." Diego pounded on his controller as red laser beams filled the screen. "You're really bad at this."

Maya tried mimicking his actions. Soon there were almost as many blue laser beams as red. "I've never played it before."

"Me neither," Diego said. "But it was a long ride from the airport."

"Diego—" Maya threw a glance in Travis's direction. He just shrugged.

“They’ll wait,” Diego said as he mowed down a line of enemy robot soldiers. “I’m worth the wait.”

Maya put down her controller. This was not the same kid she’d met down in Rio. This was a Nicole King in the making, and Maya wasn’t about to go down that path again. “Yeah, well, I’m one of the people you’ve kept waiting, and I’m not waiting anymore. I’ll be inside where it’s warm and there’s food.”

Diego’s robot exploded and the screen went dark. “Maya, hold on!” he called after her as she opened the door. “I’m sorry. I just don’t want to go to this party.”

“You think I do?” Maya said. “Welcome to the Academy.”

It was exactly the kind of thing Cleo would say and it seemed to work. Diego followed her out of the car as Travis brought up the rear. Nails greeted the three of them warmly, with the slightest uptick of a smile in her direction.

Maya stared into her punch. The electric purple color of the drink didn’t exist in nature. She suspected it was some kind of energy beverage from a company that had a special deal to force people to drink it at all Academy functions. The only other options were wine, beer, and water. She should have gone with the water.

Maya tried to figure out the point of her being at the party as she gazed into the purple void. Sure, she’d gotten Diego out of the limousine, but Nails swooped him up immediately, introducing him to his new coaches. She hadn’t talked to him since. She hadn’t talked to Travis either. None of the faculty or coaches wanted to chat, which was fine by her. She was content letting herself be hypnotized by the ripples she made in her punch.

"You're not really drinking that?" Travis asked as he took the purple concoction from her and abandoned it on an end table.

"Thank you," Maya said. "I was dying over here. Never knew you were so popular with the faculty."

"*I'm* not," Travis said. "They think if they cozy up to me, it will help them when they need something from Dad."

"That's horrible."

"Not really," Travis said. "Comes in handy when I need some extra credit."

Maya knew Travis well enough to realize he was joking. He would never exploit his relationship with his dad like that. Besides, his grades were good enough on their own. He didn't need an assist.

Maya nodded toward the other side of the room. "Looks like Diego is popular too." The soccer coaching staff had their new recruit surrounded. Diego looked about as bored as Travis had when the faculty had him cornered.

"Poor guy," Travis said. "I can't imagine that's how he planned to spend his first night here."

"Better than my welcome to the Academy sucking in bus fumes," Maya admitted.

Travis nodded. "Yeah. Dad has to work on that. We have a big welcome thing in September, but so many students are added randomly throughout the year that we should do something special for them, too. We're good about getting students to the school, but we need to work on what to do with them once they're here."

"*We?*" Maya said. "I didn't realize you work in administration."

Travis's laugh had an edge to it. "I grew up on this campus. I'm more a part of it than most of the staff."

"Is that what you want?" Maya asked. "To run this place one day?"

"That's the plan," Travis said. "I'll be a first-round draft pick, get onto a top team, have a stellar career, then retire and take over the reigns from Dad."

"But is that what you *want*?" she asked again.

"That's the plan," he repeated.

A muscular hand came down on Maya's shoulder and a matching hand landed on Travis. "Mind if I speak with the two of you for a moment?" Nails asked.

Before either of them could answer, Maya felt herself being gently steered out of the living room and into his private study. Nails closed the doors, cutting them off from the small party.

"Maya, I wanted to thank you for your help earlier getting Diego out of that limo," Nails said.

"It was nothing," Maya said. "I think he was—"

"Don't underestimate your skills at managing situations. That will come in handy as your career grows."

"Thank you," Maya said. She'd learned years ago that when adults didn't want your opinion, a simple "thank you" occasionally peppered into the conversation kept it moving along.

"I was hoping to see those management skills in practice again," Nails said. "At the Academy Exposition."

"You want me to play at the Expo?" Maya asked. The Academy Exposition was the talk of the campus. Every year, the Academy opened its doors to the public for a major exhibition in which the students played against celebrities who'd donated money to the school.

To Maya it didn't sound like much of a showcase. She'd have to hold back a lot if she played against some celeb who had never picked up a racket before. But that was beside the point. She'd get to meet celebrities. Her first Hollywood star encounter hadn't gone so well. She still had nightmares about her horrible movie audition with Peyton Smith. This was a chance to put it all behind her.

"You playing in the showcase goes without saying, after this weekend," Nails said. "But, I'd hoped for something more. I'd like you and Travis to be Student Ambassadors."

"Absolutely," Travis said without hesitation. "Thanks, Dad."

Maya wasn't sure what he was asking. "Ambassadors?"

"You'd be the public faces of the event," he explained. "Make sure everything is running smoothly. Handle any problems that come up."

Maya wasn't afraid of work, but that sounded like a major undertaking. Managing all those celebrities and their egos? To say nothing of their own classmates.

"Don't worry, Maya," Travis said. "The school publicity team is really in charge. They'll deal with all the big problems. We're just the first line of defense."

"Any real issues, you'll bring to me," Nails said. "But I'm hoping for a pair of students who can minimize the need for me to be involved."

That wasn't very reassuring. It sounded like he wanted Maya to be in charge while not giving her the power to do anything. Still, Nails had already made it clear that when the

Academy asked something, it was not her place to say no. At least, not yet. Once she was a big star like Nicole, she'd be able to decline any request she wanted, even though she knew in the back of her mind that she never would.

"Okay," Maya said. "Sounds fun."

"That's great," Nails said. "Now that that's taken care of, you two go back to the party. I've got some work to wrap up in here, but I'll be out soon."

Maya suspected that Nails was making an excuse to get away from the reception for a few minutes. She couldn't be the only one who was bored out of her mind.

As soon as they were out of the office, Travis pulled Maya into a hug. "Maya, this is awesome. Do you know how big a deal it is to be Student Ambassador?" Truly, she had no idea. "I mean, I expected Dad to ask me, but you only being here a couple months . . . Maya, you have arrived!"

Maya felt like she'd "arrived" before. She'd felt like a big shot when she was chosen to audition for that Peyton Smith movie. And see how that turned out.

As they came out of their embrace, she was surprised to see Diego right beside them. "I thought you two abandoned me," he said.

"No," Maya said. "Nails needed to talk to us."

"Let me guess," Diego said. "He wants you to make a toast in my honor just to make this whole thing more awkward and uncomfortable."

"No," Maya said. "It wasn't about you at all, actually. Nails would never ask us to make some toast like we were welcoming royalty. That's *his* job."

Travis's face scrunched up, which Maya noticed immediately. "Travis? Are you making a toast later?"

"Just a short one," Travis said. "Welcoming Diego on behalf of the students. It's not like Dad asked me to prepare a speech."

"Doesn't matter," Diego said. "I won't be here. It's my first night in the States. There's got to be a party or a club opening or something we can go to."

"360," Maya suggested, before she realized she'd spoken out loud. Nails would freak if they snuck out of the party. That was not very ambassadorial behavior. But Renee had been talking about the club ever since Maya got back. Her friends were there right now.

"We can't go to that," Travis quickly said. "We can't leave."

But Diego was already on the scent of a party. "What is a 360?"

"It's a club," she explained. "This is the only night of the week the club is open to the underage crowd."

"A teenybopper club doesn't sound that fun," Diego said.

"You've never been to an underage club here," Maya said. Not that she'd been to one either, unless she counted the Underground, which she didn't.

"Okay, Maya," Diego said. "Show me the town."

"You can't go," Travis reminded him. "This whole thing is in your honor."

"You mean *you* can't go," Diego corrected him. "I can do what I want. As you pointed out, this thing is in my honor. And I would be much more honored if my welcoming committee took me out on the town. What do you say, Maya?"

"I don't think this is a good idea," she answered honestly.

"The fun ideas are never good," Diego said. "You've served your time here. Now comes a reward."

Maya looked over at the clumps of teachers and coaches circled around in quiet conversation. It was probably the exact opposite of what Renee and Cleo were doing at that moment. If they stuck around at the reception any longer, they'd never make it to the club before it closed. It was a school night, after all.

"I'm in," she said.

Maya and Diego turned to Travis. "I can't," he said. "My dad's right on the other side of the door."

"Your dad is Nails Reed," Diego said. "The guy who got his nickname from all the women he nailed in college. That guy would want you to go out on the town."

All the air suddenly went out of the room. "That's not where his nickname comes from," Travis said through clenched teeth.

Diego shrugged it off. "All those coaches keep telling me how much you're like your dad. Maybe it's time to prove it."

Chapter 6

Maya carefully stepped out of the Porsche Cayenne Turbo, making sure that her skirt didn't ride up too high as she reached for the curb. The line to get into 360 went all the way down the block and every head turned to see who was getting out of the luxury SUV. Maya felt like she was disappointing them by failing to provide a genuine star sighting.

Diego slipped out from the backseat. He let out a long, low whistle when he saw the line. "We are never getting in tonight."

"It's okay," Maya said. "Travis is probably on some list. We'll be fine."

Maya sounded like she knew what she was talking about, but the truth was she'd only been to one other hot spot since moving to Florida. This experience was almost as foreign to her as Diego's homeland had been.

They waited on the sidewalk while Travis gave detailed instructions to the valet about the proper way to park the

SUV. He wasn't normally so specific, but it wasn't exactly his car he was about to hand over to a total stranger.

Travis's Mercedes Roadster was only a two-seater. The three of them had quickly realized that they would need an alternative mode of transportation after they slipped out of the formal reception unnoticed. Since Maya was carless and Diego's limo had gone off duty, that only left one of the rides in Nails Reed's small fleet of vehicles. Quietly slipping out of the garage in a car stolen from his dad's collection was Travis's second act of rebellion that night.

When Maya turned her attention back to the club, she was surprised to see the bouncer holding the velvet rope open for her. "Good evening, Ms. Hart. Welcome to 360."

Maya looked down at the rope, then up at the bouncer. "Excuse me?"

"Ms. Ledecq is already inside," he said. "She made sure you were on the list."

"Th-thank you." Maya stepped across the invisible line separating her from the riffraff waiting on the sidewalk. It wasn't the first time she'd gotten past a velvet rope before, but on the previous occasion she'd had Nicole King by her side.

"Impressive, Maya," Diego said as he followed. "You do know how to show off for the new guy."

They waited in the doorway beneath the neon 360 sign for Travis to catch up. "I figured there was a chance Renee put us on the list," Maya said. "But I didn't have to tell him who I was. He *recognized* me."

Diego smiled. "Of course he did. You're news. I was reading about you all the way in Rio over the weekend."

"But . . . I didn't even win." The fact that Maya had made news wasn't news to her. She'd seen the articles herself. She just didn't think anyone else had.

"Why are you hanging out in the doorway?" Travis asked when he finally caught up to them.

"Maya wanted to make sure you could get in," Diego joked. "Since we're clearly not celebrities like her."

"Speak for yourself." Travis took Maya's arm. "I'm the son of Nails Reed, football hero. That makes me famous by association. . . . Able to get into clubs across this nation . . . so long as the owners remember my dad."

Maya laughed along with Diego even though she thought that she'd heard an unusual touch of bitterness beneath the joke. She expected that type of attitude from a different Reed brother, not Travis. Brushing it aside as a figment of her imagination, Maya walked through the doorway and into an entirely different world.

The club was thumping. Music pounded out of the speakers and lights danced along to the pulsing beat. Bodies filled every inch of the floor. Most were moving to the rhythm, but a few were completely out of step and didn't seem to care at all.

Maya made quite an entrance walking in on the arm of a hot guy. Sure, they were only friends, but the girls shooting her jealous looks as they watched the door didn't know that.

The good feeling lasted for about a half second. Then she saw the other brother heading their way.

"What's the matter?" Travis asked as she pulled away from

him. He held on tighter, unaware that his brother was coming toward them. "It's okay. Friends can hang on to each other's arms. It doesn't mean anything."

"No," Maya said. "It's—"

"I thought you two had some official hosting duties tonight. Did Dad give you a 'get out of fancy reception free' card or something?" Jake may have been speaking to both of them, but his eyes never once looked to Maya. If only the same could be said for other eyes in the club.

The death glares Maya now got from the girls scoping the entrance almost caused her to laugh out loud. If only those girls knew the truth. Maya was standing with three of the hottest guys in the club, but it was the last place she wanted to be.

Travis clung even more tightly to Maya. "We skipped out early. Diego wanted to see the town."

"Diego?" Jake asked, noticing the third wheel for the first time. "You the new competition?"

"I thought the Reed brothers played American football," Diego said. "Not the real thing."

"Oh, we play the real thing, all right," Jake said. "Not some lame version of kickball."

"And why do you need those helmets? To protect your hairdos?" Diego asked, coming chest to chest with Jake.

"Hey!" Travis jumped in. "My stylist charges two hundred fifty dollars for this look. I have to protect my investment."

The guys busted up laughing, breaking the tension. Funny how Jake could joke around with his brother, but still couldn't bring himself to look at Maya.

"We'll set you up at the salon sometime." Jake reached for Diego's head. "She could do wonders with those dark curly locks."

Diego ducked out of the way. "Thanks, man."

Jake held out a hand. "Nice to meet you, Diego. I look forward to beating you on the field of battle. Just name the sport."

"Poker," Diego said as they shook. "That's my favorite sport. So, did you come over to buy us drinks?"

"Nope," Jake said. "Time to go. I have practice in the morning."

Maya was glad that Travis had her arm. She about fell over when Jake said that he was leaving a club early because of practice.

Jake finally noticed Maya. "I never had the chance to congratulate you," he said, holding out a hand to her. "Nice game this weekend."

Maya untangled herself from Travis so she could shake Jake's hand. It was warm and inviting, with just the right amount of pressure. "Thank you. Have a good practice."

"Thanks," he said as he left. Just like that. He *left*. No posturing. No strained conversation with his brother. He was polite to Maya, but remote. And it didn't seem to have anything to do with her hanging on to Travis's arm.

Maya couldn't help but notice that no one was hanging on to Jake's arm.

Diego put his hands on Maya's shoulders and pushed her into the crowd. "Okay, Maya," he whisper-yelled into her ear over the thumping music of the club. "Since you already have enough guys after you, I think it's time you introduced me to some girls before I have to make my move, too."

Maya laughed at the joke. At least, she hoped it was a joke. He was right about that. She was already dealing with more guys than she could handle.

Maya was so glad she'd blown off the reception, she didn't even care if it meant another call to Nails Reed's office. The playlist at 360 was great, the drinks were tasty, and, best of all, everyone was having a blast. She'd been most worried about that last part. Cleo was still mad at Travis for the role he played in Nicole's plan to break up Maya and Jake. It didn't matter that Cleo believed he wasn't a completely willing participant. She was angry that he would fall for one of Nicole's schemes.

To be fair, Cleo was even angrier with Jake for believing it. That was the great thing about Cleo—she always had Maya's back.

Renee was the most easygoing of the trio, so she'd embraced Travis as part of the group more easily than even Maya, who still had her suspicions. Renee also embraced Diego, but that had more to do with his strong biceps, sexy accent, and piercing eyes.

Maya enjoyed watching Renee get her flirt on. She'd seen it before, but this show was different. Diego's skills were on par with Renee's, if not better. It was a master class in flirtation, and Maya had a front-row seat.

"Why don't you want to dance?" Renee asked Diego with a pout that implied she was waiting to be asked.

"I save my moves for the soccer field," he replied.

"Shame to waste those moves on a field full of other guys," she countered.

"Well, I keep some moves for more private shows," he said.

Maya and Cleo both downed the last of their drinks. The master class had turned from an entertaining display to a personal moment, and it was clear they both felt they'd crossed the line from playful eavesdroppers to voyeurs.

"Excuse me," Cleo said. "But that girl's had her eye on me all evening, and it's time I did something about it."

A tall, long-haired girl with an exotic look and multiple piercings was watching Cleo. She smiled as Cleo started toward her. Maya was glad that her friends had each found someone, but it suddenly made her being alone with her one other *friend* a lot more uncomfortable.

"Another drink?" Travis asked.

Maya picked the drink menu off the bar. The club specialized in crazy, colorful concoctions that blended fruit juices into works of art so much better than that mysterious purple punch at the reception. None of the drinks had alcohol, but the sugar content was so high, they didn't need any liquor.

Maya worked her way down the list of silly tropical names. She'd already tried a Mango Melon Breeze, a Coconut Beach Comber, a Sunset Slammer, and a Banana Cabana. "I'm in the mood for"—her finger slid down the list—"blue!"

Travis laughed. "Blue it is." He flagged down the bartender and ordered a True Blue Hawaii for each of them.

"I'm getting these." Maya reached for her purse. The drinks were expensive, but she had enough to pay for this round.

"Don't worry," Travis said. "It's covered."

"Travis, if we're going to be friends, I can't let you pay for everything. How would that be fair?"

It wouldn't be fair, but it was more complicated than that. Travis could afford to buy a round of drinks for everyone in the club. Maya would be scrounging change out of the bottom of her bag just to pay for the two of them. Someday, maybe, she'd be in the position to shout "Drinks on me!" to the cheers of the crowd. But today was not that day.

"Don't worry, Maya," Travis said. "I'm not trying to impress you again. When I say it's covered, I mean that Renee opened a tab. She got everything we ordered tonight. Or, her *parents* covered our drinks. I think she's still mad at them for missing her last swim meet."

That explained why Renee had insisted on that round of Sunset Slammers, the drinks with the gold flecks in them. Even without liquor, the Slammers were the most expensive thing on the menu. Between the five of them, Renee had already spent well over two hundred dollars on refreshments. Maya had never paid that much for a *meal*. It was weird to think that someday that could be the norm if she continued on the path she'd planned for herself.

Thinking about that kind of future brought her mind back to Jordan's offer. Maya always knew that she'd need an agent one day. She just hadn't expected that day to come so fast. She didn't expect the drinks to come that fast either. The tall glasses full of blue, ice-blended decadence were suddenly on the bar in front of them.

Travis picked them up and handed Maya her drink. "To friendship," he said, raising his glass.

“To friendship,” she agreed.

The blue slushy drink was cold and smooth running down her throat. It was the tastiest drink so far. She enjoyed it so much that she had to remind herself to sip rather than chug. She might not have to worry about a hangover, but she was concerned about a brain freeze.

“That’s good.” Travis put his glass down on the bar next to Maya’s. “Better go slow on these, though.”

“I was just thinking the same thing.”

“No, you’re thinking about something else,” he said. “Something important. You have that look in your eyes. What’s on your mind?”

Maya wasn’t sure she should tell Travis about the offer. Since Cleo had been there when Jordan made it, they’d had to tell Renee to be fair. They didn’t like keeping secrets in their friendship. They’d agreed that it shouldn’t go any further than the three of them, though. They didn’t want to risk Nicole finding out.

Travis had more experience in this area than any of them. He didn’t have an agent yet, but he’d been around his father’s business stuff all his life. Then again, Travis was friends with Nicole, and Maya was afraid of this getting back to her. But if they really were going to be friends, she’d have to start out by trusting him.

“Okay,” Maya said, more to herself than to Travis. “But you can’t tell anyone. Not even your father.”

“Maya, I don’t tell my dad *everything*,” he said.

Maya wasn’t so sure about that, but she told Travis the story about how Jordan “randomly” bumped into her anyway.

It wasn't nearly as exciting a retelling as it had been when Renee kept jumping in with gossipy questions. It just sounded like a simple business transaction, which it probably was.

"That's incredible," Travis said. "Dad's been pushing his agent to represent me for a while now, but he keeps pushing back. Says it's 'too early.' I haven't even gotten an official college offer yet. That's if I decide not to go straight to the pros."

"So, you think I should do it?"

"I didn't say that." Travis took a sip of his drink while he thought over her situation. "It's good that you've got interest from an agent. But if there's one, there are probably others. You have to figure out who comes with the best offer."

"Like someone not representing the girl who wants to wipe the courts with me? Or completely wipe me off the courts?"

Travis shook his head. "A good agent keeps her clients separate. You don't have to worry about something like that with Jordan. I mean, you should be *aware* of it, but don't let that be the deciding factor."

Maya sucked on a sliver of ice. Travis hadn't said much, but he gave her a lot to consider. The problem with talking to Cleo and Renee was that they'd both focused on the scandalous part of Nicole's agent asking to represent Maya. But Travis was right. Jordan represented several clients. Why should any of them get in the way of Maya's plans?

By the time Maya finished her second blue drink, she'd forgotten all about Jordan's offer and was entirely focused on Travis. This friendship thing was fun. She didn't spend all her time worrying about impressing him or saying the right thing or even wondering what his motivations were. She wasn't even thinking about kissing him, although his blue-tinted lips were kind of cute.

Okay, maybe she was thinking a little bit about kissing him.

Cleo's yell brought an abrupt end to that thought. "Maya! It's almost curfew!"

Maya grabbed Travis's arm and looked at his watch. They only had fifteen minutes to make the ten-minute drive back to campus. Add in the time it would take to work their way out of the crowded club and wait in line for the valet, and they were pushing it. "We've got to go."

"It's okay, girls," Renee said. "We're cool. I blow curfew all the time. Nobody cares. Cleo, go back to that girl on the dance floor. She looks lonely without you."

Maya calmed down. Renee was right. She'd missed curfew once before and hadn't even gotten a slap on the wrist.

"No," Cleo insisted. "We've got to go. I'm not the daughter of an ambassador, the son of the school owner, the newest 'it boy' on campus, or the up-and-coming tennis star. Curfew means something different for me."

There was no anger in Cleo's accusation. She was just stating the facts. But it bothered Maya all the same.

"You won the Invitational," Maya reminded her. "If anyone here is an up-and-coming sports star, it's you."

"And yet, nobody's inviting me to private receptions," Cleo said.

Maya relented. "Okay, we should go. We can always continue our night on campus. Although Cleo won't be able to bring her new friend."

"No worries." Cleo held up her cell phone. "I got her digits. You don't really think I'd just pull a Cinderella because the clock struck curfew, do you?"

The girls laughed as they made their way through the club. En route to the exit, it was agreed that Diego would ride back with Renee and Cleo, leaving Maya alone with Travis and his pouty blue lips.

As they exited into the cool night air, Maya wasn't surprised to find Travis's arm wrapped around her again. It felt more natural now that they were friends talking about the kinds of things she talked about with her other friends.

Travis held the door open for her as she climbed into the car, waving to the cameras that flashed all around her as if she were a real celebrity.

Chapter 7

"Oh. My. Frickin'. Goddess!"

Maya looked up from her history textbook. She'd been trying to fit in some extra homework before classes. She was still behind due to her week at the Open and her impressive social schedule. Cleo's outburst caused her to lose her place in her reading, but that wasn't important. A stage-five freak-out was happening on the other side of the dorm room.

"I'm on the Wall!" Cleo's hands waved wildly toward her computer screen. "I'm on the frickin' Wall!"

"Oh, Cleo," Maya said. "I'm so sorry."

The Wall was a gossip site that followed all the hottest of the hot in movies, TV, and music. Occasionally a sports celeb made it onto the site, like that one time Maya found herself providing a little extra color for a story about Nicole. She wasn't looking forward to repeating that experience.

"Whatever," Cleo said. "Oh, I know I'm supposed to be

above these gossip rags, but it's totally different when you see a picture of yourself in an article that's already gotten thousands and thousands of page views. That's pretty sweet. I'm on the frickin' Wall!"

Maya forced a smile. "Well, that's wonderful, Cleo. About time someone noticed your accomplishments. You deserve some press."

"Thanks," Cleo said. "But the article's not about me. I'm just in the background of the picture. My name isn't even mentioned."

"Then what . . ." A feeling of dread crept over Maya as she recalled those flashing cameras from the night before. She'd been so naïve to wave at them thinking the photographers were on the prowl for a real celebrity. "Please tell me it's an article about a hot new soccer stud from Rio."

"Oh, no," Cleo said. "This one is about American sports royalty: the football prince and his new lady love."

Maya didn't want to see the article, but she had to find out what people were writing about her. Homework was forgotten for the moment, and probably for the rest of the day. She reluctantly took the four long, difficult steps across the room to look at the screen of Cleo's computer.

A big picture of Maya and Travis walking arm in arm out of 360 was at the top of the page. Cleo and Renee were in the background. What looked to be Diego's arm made it into the picture as well. There was no doubt who the stars of the article were by the way the camera was angled for maximum couple-itude. And if there was any doubt, the article below it dashed that right away, beginning with the headline:

FOOTBALL PRINCE WITH TENNIS PAUPER.

Ouch.

The entire article seemed to be created solely around the photo. The writer managed to find a surprising amount of information about Maya, particularly that she was a scholarship student at the Academy. It made a lot of assumptions from that fact alone, building a *Romeo and Juliet* type of story about two teens from different worlds. Maya's family had always struggled with money, but she never thought of herself as *poor.* But calling her lower middle class didn't get page views, apparently.

"That's so dumb," Maya said. "Romeo and Juliet were both rich."

"So not the point, Maya," Cleo said. "You've gone mainstream media. I wouldn't be surprised if more agents started jumping out from behind bushes to offer you representation on the way to class."

Cleo's wild imagination aside, Maya knew that she should be excited. This was part of what she'd been dreaming of for years. Success and fame went hand in hand. It just felt cheaper since she hadn't even had any real success yet.

None of that really bothered her. This was the second time the Wall linked her with a Reed brother she wasn't currently dating. She didn't like that people she'd never met were investing page space in stories putting them together. She was especially bothered to see that complete strangers were already commenting on it beneath the article.

But she was particularly concerned about Jake.

. . .

The morning turned out to be an exact replica of the first time Maya appeared on the Wall. Total strangers smiled at her and waved hello as she made her way across campus. More people congratulated her about the article than had about the Open. It was as if being on the Wall was somehow a better accomplishment than a good game at a midlevel tournament. That said a lot about priorities at the Academy.

It was all a little much for Maya to deal with. She was glad that she had a practice match scheduled on the court. There was no better way to clear her head than by smashing that small rubber ball at an opponent on the other side of the net.

It was her first real practice since the tournament and Maya was on fire. Her legs were fully functional once again—no pain, no strain—and nothing got past her. Not a slice. Not a lob. Nothing.

Maya was all over the court. If the ball dropped short of the net, Maya was there. A high, overhead shot? No problem. Every single time, she slammed it back with force. Her mind was clear of everything but the ball.

Maya's sparring partner, Lindsey Jacobs, hopped the net and was standing in front of Maya before she even realized the match was over.

"That was incredible!" Lindsey said. "Normally, I hate to lose. I mean, who doesn't hate to lose? But you creamed me. On the bright side, I can now say the girl who held her own against Donata Zajacova punished me in our game."

"What?" Maya didn't even know what Lindsey was saying as the girl continued to ramble on about everything under the Florida sun. It came out so rushed, like she was racing to get in everything she could before Maya left. All Maya could make out was "Blah, blah, blah, story on the Wall!"

Was this what Maya sounded like when she first met Nicole? But Maya had known Lindsey for weeks now. They'd grabbed frozen yogurts after practice together a couple times. She never talked like that before.

"I mean, you squashed me," Lindsey continued. "You scored point after point, and I was stuck on love."

"What?" *Stuck on love* was such a funny little phrase, but Lindsey was right. She hadn't scored a single point.

Maya hadn't even noticed. Just like she hadn't noticed the small crowd of classmates that had gathered to watch their game; that were still hanging by the other side of the fence.

Suddenly, all the million things that had been crowding Maya's mind came flooding back. Jordan. Travis. Jake. The Wall. Everything. It didn't help that Lindsey wouldn't shut up.

"Thank you," Maya said, when she just wanted to tell Lindsey to get over it. Maya was hyperaware that she had to be kind even though she had an overwhelming desire to get out of there. She didn't want anyone confusing her with Nicole.

After enduring a few more gushing tributes, Maya excused herself as politely as she could and left the court. She wanted to be alone, but she needed something to drink. Water wouldn't be enough to restock the electrolytes she'd lost in that game. She knew she should get away from the area, but nothing would quench her thirst like one of the energy drinks they served at the café beside the courts, aptly named Slice.

Heads turned to see who'd come into the café, and everyone lingered a bit longer than usual when they saw it was Maya.

While all the attention in the place was aimed at Maya, she was focused on someone else: Nicole. Oddly, the most popular girl in school sat alone, hunched over like she didn't want to be disturbed. Nicole must have spent some time cultivating that pose of casual indifference. It was rare to see her without a pack of admirers.

Maya discreetly eyed Nicole. The tennis star held her icy drink against the same wrist she'd nursed while she put makeup on after her match.

Nicole was casual about it. The drink just seemed to be resting there. She certainly didn't look like she was icing her wrist. But to Maya it was as bright as a neon sign on a dark country road. It had been days since the tournament and she was still in pain. That wasn't good.

Nicole raised her drink and their eyes met. Without a word, Nicole slammed down her cup and stood, making a quick exit. She wasn't embarrassed or ashamed. She was mad. Maya knew her secret. And it was going to cost her.

Maya sat with her drink at a table in the corner doing her best to adopt Nicole's unwelcoming pose. The last thing she wanted was for anyone to think she was like her former idol, but she had to admit it worked. Everyone backed off, which gave her some time to consider what to do about Nicole.

It was crazy that Nicole hadn't seen a doctor about her wrist. That much was obvious since it wasn't wrapped and cold drinks weren't exactly the best way to ice an injury. *But why?* The next major tournament was weeks away. She had plenty of time to heal. If anything, Nicole could use the injury as an excuse for why she hadn't played that well against Dona. Bloggers still gave her a hard time for not crushing Dona. It was a completely unfair accusation, but Nicole was never afraid to milk the media for attention. An injury would be the perfect way to change the story.

Before coming to the Academy, Maya never thought of ways "to change the story." This wasn't exactly the kind of education she'd expected to receive at the school. But it was certainly useful—especially if Maya kept winding up on the Wall.

She had to tell Jordan. No one else was closer to Nicole. The agent could always pretend that she noticed some of the same things Maya had. Nicole had to be showing all kinds of signs that someone with Jordan's experience would be able to flag.

As the answer came to Maya, Jordan conveniently did as well. A warm blast of air announced the café door opening again. The agent came in and made a beeline for Maya, ignoring her body language. Since it was Nicole's pose to begin with, Maya suspected that Jordan had a lot of practice with it.

Maya had always been a "rip off the Band-Aid" kind of girl. As soon as she invited Jordan to sit with her, she got right to the point. "I need to talk to you about Nicole."

"I suspected you might," Jordan said, surprising Maya. "I realize you two aren't best friends, but you're both professionals now. You won't be the first clients I've had who didn't get along. This is business, Maya, not high school."

"No," Maya said. "It's not that." Although that subject also bothered her. It was kind of weird for Jordan to say something like that while they sat in the middle of a high school. Sure, it was a high school with manicured grounds, Olympic-style training facilities, and a mall's worth of shops and cafés, but a high school nonetheless.

"You have nothing to worry about," Jordan insisted. "I don't play favorites. And I don't pit my clients against one another. You and Nicole are two completely different personalities. I will set you up with opportunities befitting those personalities."

That was certainly nice to hear, but seriously, if Jordan wasn't going to let her get a word in edgewise, Maya might have to go with another agent. She needed someone she could work with, not someone who would steamroll over her.

"But I'm not here to discuss Nicole," Jordan said.

"But—"

"I have an offer for you." Jordan continued to steamroll away. "Well, not an offer per se, but a potential offer. You've heard about Esteban's new line of designer sportswear, right?"

"Um . . . no." Maya had heard of Esteban, of course. He designed half the dresses on the Oscars' red carpet. But Maya didn't follow fashion news enough to know what he was currently working on.

"Oh, well, it has been kind of hush-hush," Jordan said. "Anyway, the ad agency working with Esteban is in need of a fresh-faced sporting model for the ad campaign. Your name came up when I was speaking with my contact this morning. I suspect it had something to do with that piece on the Wall. Good placement, by the way. Did you do that?"

"Did I do what?"

"Tip off the photogs that you'd be at that club with Travis?"

"No." Maya didn't even know how to get in touch with a "photog."

Jordan slapped a hand down on the table. "Great! That means you're happening organically. Love that. Esteban will, too. He's a little on the eccentric side, but you won't meet him till later. First there's the go-see."

"Go-see?"

Jordan picked up her phone and started texting. Maya hated when people did that. "They just want to take a look at you. Maybe get a few test shots. Go to this address tomorrow after class. They're expecting you at four."

Maya's cell phone buzzed in her purse. She didn't normally check her texts in the middle of a conversation, but she had a feeling that buzz had something to do with the address Jordan had mentioned.

She was right. Jordan had texted her. *But how had the agent gotten her phone number?*

Jordan was out of her seat before Maya could even formulate a full question. "Sorry about the hit and run, but I'm working a deal for . . . Well, I can't tell you." She giggled like she'd already said too much. It was awkward and completely fake, but Maya appreciated the attempt.

"I know I just threw a lot at you," Jordan said, "but I wouldn't do that if I didn't think you could handle it. And don't feel like you have to go with me just because I found this opportunity for you. Consider it a gift in contemplation of a future relationship. If you decide you'd be a better fit with another agent, just remember to thank me at the SNC Awards show when you're voted player of the year. Talk more later."

"Bye," Maya said to the empty spot that Jordan had already left behind.

Chapter 8

Maya tried to get into her homework, but she couldn't concentrate. Her mind was still reeling from her conversation with Jordan, and Cleo couldn't get off the topic either.

"It's probably part of her pitch," Cleo said as she painted her nails alternately black and gray. "She comes in, drops off a huge opportunity, then disappears before you can think or ask a question. As long as she keeps moving, she keeps you on your toes."

"Like a shark," Maya said. "They have to keep moving or they die."

"Probably," Cleo agreed. "Just watch out she doesn't get you in her teeth."

"You think she could be out to get me? Like Nicole put her up to this?"

"No," Cleo said. "She's a sports agent. She knows a good deal when she sees one. You, my friend, are a good deal. At least you are this week. She's got the inside track because she knows you. A few more articles on the Wall and another tournament will bring her competition out of the woodwork."

"The Skyborne Cup is still a while away. She's not going to hold out that long." Maya had signed up for the tournament first thing Monday morning. If Donata Zajacova said she should be there, that was enough for Maya.

"No, she's going to force a decision before that," Cleo said. "In the meantime, she's giving you a freebie. That doesn't happen, like, *ever.* Take it. See how it goes."

"Yeah, but if I book the shoot, I'll feel like I owe her," Maya said. "Like I have to sign with her."

Cleo shrugged. "Maybe, maybe not. If you're chosen as the face of Esteban's new sportswear line, that will get your name out there faster than the cup. You could start fielding offers as early as next week."

Maya didn't even want to think about that. She'd been working on her tennis game since she was seven. That kind of success she was ready for. This other side to the business was completely foreign to her. She definitely needed someone with more experience on her side. But was Jordan Cromwell that person?

Maya still needed to catch up on her homework, but as soon as she woke her laptop she somehow found herself on the Internet. She wanted to know more about Jordan. All she had on the woman so far was her relationship with Nicole, and that wasn't a good indicator of anything.

Maya typed Jordan's name into a Google search and hit the mother lode. Jordan was even bigger than Maya suspected.

Only two of the hits on the first page were tied to Nicole. Jordan represented athletes across all sports.

The majority of Jordan's clients were female sports figures. Maya liked that. Women didn't generally make the same kind of money as men in sports, so it was nice to know someone as successful as Jordan was still focused on female clients. At the same time, Maya was concerned that she'd be competing with Jordan's other clients for the same jobs.

Jordan was just one part of a large sports agency. She'd be Maya's point person, but she also oversaw a team of agents that specialized in different fields. Jordan was the ultimate deal maker, but the junior agents did the legwork. There were agents for modeling gigs, sneaker endorsements, and even reality shows. They'd set the clients up and Jordan would knock them out of the park.

It felt a bit like a conveyor belt to Maya. She'd be just another product at a big agency like that. What she gained in the power of a team, she would lose in the personal touch. That mattered to her.

After pages and pages of searches, Maya was even more confused than she'd been when she started. This was the real world. She had to make a decision that could impact the rest of her life. And then she had to finish her chemistry homework.

But first, she typed her own name into the Google search.

Google roulette was a dangerous pastime. Maya started this game when her first picture went up on the Wall a couple of weeks back. She never knew when she'd come across a link that she'd rather not see. Like that girl on Twitter a few weeks ago who had a crush on Jake Reed and was writing horrible things about Maya.

"Hart" wasn't exactly a unique last name. It was kind of disappointing the first few times she played it to find that so many other Maya Harts came up before her.

It wasn't like that anymore.

Every Maya Hart on the first page of the search was her. There were articles about her match against Dona, photos of her at the press conference, and, of course, a ton of stuff about her and Travis at 360. Most of it was nice. Some of it was not. One thing in particular was really, really bad.

"Ummm."

Cleo looked up from her nails. "Um, what?"

Maya wanted to say "Um, nothing," but that wouldn't be fair to Cleo. She had to know. "Grant Adams is writing about you again."

Cleo looked wary. "What more could he possibly have to write about me? Savannah was days ago."

"Not Savannah. A little closer. A lot more recent."

"What?" The springs on Cleo's bed were still squeaking when she reached Maya and elbowed her out of the way to read the article. This one had very little to do with golf and everything to do with that one picture on the Wall with Cleo in the background.

"Party girl? He's calling me a party girl? I don't even go to parties unless you and Renee drag me there."

"I'm so sorry," Maya said. If people hadn't been taking pictures of her, no one would have even known Cleo was out at the club.

"I'm not sorry. I'm mad. This bozo thinks he can get away with this?" Cleo's fingers tapped across the keyboard. Even in her anger, she was careful not to get nail polish on the keys.

"Cleo, what are you doing?"

"Telling him what I think about some old man picking on a teenage girl."

"Cleo, stop. You can't do that."

Her fingers never slowed. Maya read the comment as Cleo wrote. It was actually a pretty good takedown. The wording was calm and reasoned, no matter how emotional Cleo's fast fingers made it seem. But Cleo getting involved was going to turn it into a big deal.

"Cleo!"

"Too late." She posted the comment. "Don't worry. It's anonymous."

Maya confirmed that the comment had gone up with "Anonymous" as the writer, but she still wasn't so sure it was a great idea. These things had a way of spiraling out of control. In the seconds since Cleo posted, there was already one response to Cleo's comment.

Maya had to grab Cleo to keep her from writing back, smearing nail polish all over both their hands.

Maya tried to keep her mind on chemistry, but her computer somehow kept flipping back to Cleo's article. Cleo's single comment had started a flame war with people agreeing with and attacking Grant Adams for going after a teenage girl. Thankfully, Cleo had stayed out of it since posting her initial comment. She was back on her bed fixing her nails. But Maya was pretty sure the article had an impact on Cleo, since she'd been working on the same finger for the past ten minutes.

Pounding on their dorm room door made them both jump. It was loud and intense—the kind of banging that usually meant the building was on fire or some other catastrophe had happened.

"Maya! Cleo! Let me in!" Renee pleaded.

Maya flew to the door and opened it, panicked that something major had happened. She was surprised to see Renee casually leaning against the doorframe, as if she hadn't just been trying to break down their door. "Hey. How's it going?"

Maya shared a confused look with Cleo. "Fine. And you?"

Renee slipped into the room. "Oh, you know. Nothing exciting. Thought I'd stop by and say hi."

Cleo rolled her eyes. "Slumming it in the dorms twice in one week? Nice try. What's wrong?"

"Aren't you supposed to be on a date with Diego?" Maya asked. She hadn't been surprised that either of her friends had moved that fast, but it was a shock that the evening had ended so early. It was barely nine.

Renee was unusually quiet.

"That bad?" Cleo sat beside Renee on Maya's bed, blowing on her fingernails to dry them faster.

"It was the worst date I've ever been on. And I've gone on a lot of dates."

Maya sat on the other side of Renee. "Tell."

Renee sighed. "Okay, so Diego's new to the city, right? I told him I was going to take him out on the town and show him the sights. I used my dad's name to get us into Violetta—I mean, Dad's got to be useful for something and that is like the hottest new restaurant in the city. It started out fine, but that banter thing we had going on at the club the other night wasn't there. Seriously, by the appetizer we were pretty much sitting in silence.

"So, I figured Italian isn't his thing," she continued. "We hit up that fancy chocolatier, Dulce, next for dessert. I mean, what guy says no to dessert? But I guess he's on some strict diet or something because he didn't touch the huge slice of caramel chocolate cake we got. And, you know I wasn't eating it either, so it sat there between us while we stared at it. Then he took me home and didn't even want to come in. And Nicole was totally out for the night. I don't know what I did wrong. I mean, me? At a loss for words with a guy? What's that about?"

Maya shared a look with Cleo behind Renee's back. Maya knew exactly what was wrong. "Sounds like you might have been trying too hard," she suggested. "Travis did the same thing on our first date. Diego's not used to fine dining and chocolatiers."

"Trying too hard? I wasn't trying anything. That's a typical date for me. Okay, I did pay, but that's only because it was my idea."

"And it was on your parents' cards," Cleo suggested.

"Exactly."

Maya shared another glance with Cleo behind Renee's back. "Renee, you know what kind of background Diego comes from, right?"

"Oh, I get that," Renee said. "I can deal with a guy who's weird about me paying. I can usually play that stuff off. But no guy has ever ended the night with me before. I'm the one who tells him when it's over. And that's not even the worst part."

Maya was officially confused. "What is?"

Renee let out another deep sigh. She wasn't often a drama queen, but her royal act was in overdrive. "*I care!*"

"Okay?" Maya and Cleo said in unison.

"I don't usually *care*," Renee said. "I've had bad dates before. And, okay, this was like the *worst* of the worst. But usually I just chalk it up to the guy and move on. Girls, I'm not moving on. I want to know what I did wrong. I want to fix it. I want to go out with him again even though I might come out of a second date looking even more pathetic."

The final look Maya shared with Cleo behind Renee's back had them both smiling. They didn't enjoy taking pleasure in their friend's pain, but it was kind of nice to see the most confident one of their trio with a slight crack in her cool demeanor.

"That's not a bad thing," Maya said. "It means you like him."

"Like, you *like him*, like him," Cleo added.

"You like him a lot," Maya continued in a sing-songy voice.

"Oh my God," Renee said. "I think I do."

Chapter 9

Maya was no stranger to pain. In the years she'd been playing tennis she suffered through blisters, strains, sprains, and more serious injuries earned from her time on the court. None of that pain compared to the agony of wearing a pair of Ottaviano shoes. They were the most uncomfortable footwear she'd ever encountered, including the walking brace she had to wear for a month in seventh grade.

Maya sat in the empty lobby of the Creative Core Ad Agency dressed entirely in borrowed clothes. She had developed such a pattern of borrowing Renee's clothes that she considered offering to pay rent.

Renee had great taste and was much more knowledgeable about this world. Maya had wanted to dress in Esteban from head to toe, but Renee stopped her. The famous designer's labels filled Renee's closet, but she wouldn't let her friend take any of it. "Too obvious," she'd said.

Once Renee was done with her, Maya was outfitted in a Michael Kors dress, a Cartier Tank watch, a Chanel bag, and those hideously uncomfortable but ultimately gorgeous heels. Only then did Renee reach back into her closet and top off the look with an Esteban scarf that complemented the outfit perfectly. The one outfit cost more than Maya's wardrobe budget for the whole year, but she looked good sitting in that lobby. If only someone other than the receptionist would see her in it.

Maya had been waiting for an hour with no sign she was going to be seen anytime soon. She'd be annoyed, but she was too busy trying not to throw up.

They'd never keep Nicole King waiting this long, she told herself. Nicole would never put up with it. She'd have been gone long ago.

Maya considered getting up and walking out. Since she was effectively a nobody, there was no chance she'd book the job, but it would send a message. *Maya Hart doesn't wait for anyone.*

She'd never do something like that, but it was fun to imagine. The shadow that suddenly fell over her told her she didn't need to think about it anymore. She put on her brightest smile and raised her head.

"What are *you* doing here?"

Travis's smile was as bright as her own. "Wow. That was not the greeting I expected."

"Sorry," Maya sputtered. "But . . . what *are* you doing here? Did Jordan send you for moral support?"

Travis slid in next to her on the leather bench. "What do you need moral support for? You're going to be great."

"Thank you. But why are you here?"

"I'm up for the ad, too," he said. "Jordan mentioned it to Dad after she told you about it. They're looking for a girl and a guy for the campaign. He arranged it for me. I didn't say anything because I wanted to surprise you when you got out of the audition. How did it go?"

"It hasn't gone yet," she said. "I'm still waiting."

"Really? Wow. That's incredibly unprofessional. Let me check in and see if we can do something about that." Travis stood back up.

"Travis, no."

He shook her off. "It's okay, Maya. I'm not going to cause a scene. I'm just going to let them know I'm here."

Maya watched as Travis sauntered away. Questions flooded her mind as the old doubts came back in. Was Travis using her for this opportunity? Is that what their friendship was about? She worried that there were already plans for them to be the next big media couple. Traya? Mavis?

There was no doubt in her mind that Nails liked them together for that reason, but Travis was still an unknown. He had as much right to try out for the campaign as she did. And it wasn't like they'd be competing against each other. It was kind of nice to have his friendly face around.

Even looking at him from behind, Maya could tell he was flashing that bright Reed smile on his walk to the reception desk. She couldn't hear what he said to the receptionist, but the woman looked a lot happier than she had the entire time Maya sat in the lobby. Maya envied his charm. She feared it as well.

The receptionist picked up her phone and made a quick

call while Travis returned to Maya. By the time he'd reached the leather bench, a door to the right of the reception desk opened and a frantic-looking man hurried out. He introduced himself simply as Steven and told them to follow him.

"I'm so sorry we kept you waiting, Ms. Hart," Steven said. "And thank you for coming by, too, Mr. Reed. We had a minor crisis this afternoon, but it's been resolved. Since we're at the end of the day, I hope you two won't mind sharing the meeting?"

"Not a problem," Travis said. "We're old friends."

"Fine with me," Maya agreed. So far, their friendship was coming in handy.

"That's great, Maya," Steven said as the camera flashed away. "Now try for a smile that's a little less . . . strained."

Maya relaxed her smile as much as she could. Her face didn't feel strained to her. The rest of her body, however, was an uncoordinated mess. She really wished that she'd worn her own clothing. It might not have looked as good as Renee's, but she would have been more comfortable.

The problem began at the shoes, then worked its way up to include everything else she had on. Maya simply didn't know how to move in the outfit. It was easy to blame the clothes, but the truth was, it was the camera. And all the people behind the camera.

Steven, who she'd come to learn was an executive assistant, worked the camera for the test shots. He was friendly enough, but his frantic nature did nothing to calm her nerves no matter how soothing his words. Steven's boss and a half-dozen agency executives sat at a long table behind Steven, whispering to one another while she posed.

The initial interview had gone well. With Travis by her side, it was more like a casual conversation. They were looking for "fresh faces," which Maya was happy to learn just meant "amateurs." Models didn't come much more amateur than her.

The executives had been engaging when they talked about Maya's recent tournament and the buzz about Travis on the field. Although Maya was "Maya" through the entire discussion, they kept calling Travis "Reed." It wasn't unusual to call a football player by his last name, but it sounded weird since they never called her "Hart."

Maya stopped going over the interview in her head and tried to focus on the posing. Steven continued to snap away while he gave instructions. "Try to look like you're having . . . you know . . . fun."

Maya tried, but this was the least fun she'd had in her life. Every pose felt faker than the last. Balancing on heels with one arm out toward the camera and a seductive expression on her face didn't exactly scream "Ready to hit the courts."

"I think we're good," one of the executives said, finally. Maya thanked everyone, then sat in an empty seat beside Travis on the side of the room.

"Your turn," she said quietly to him through a forced smile.

"Don't know that I'll be able to beat that, but I'll do my best."

"Flatterer," she said. "Lying flatterer."

He patted her on the cheek. "Just wait to see how bad I can do."

Travis was actually pretty good at modeling. His poses came across naturally. He seemed comfortable in front of the camera. It made sense, since he'd grown up in the public eye. He was born at the height of Nails's career, when the media was interested in every aspect of the superstar's life. A simple Google search netted enough pictures of Nails and his children to make a scrapbook for each year of the boys' lives.

Maya was glad to be off to the side of the room. With Steven positioned between her and Travis, she had a pretty good view of what the executives saw. She was also close enough to hear a whisper that came out a bit louder than one executive probably anticipated.

"Reed's got a good look, but there's nothing behind the eyes."

The two executives on either side of the bad whisperer nodded in agreement. Maya tried to see what they meant, but she didn't have a clue. Travis's eyes looked like they always did: hazel with tiny flecks of green and perfectly adorable.

She shook herself out of it. That wasn't the way friends thought about each other.

Maya felt like she'd been up there for hours, but Travis only went a few minutes before one of the nameless execs said, "Thanks, Reed. You can sit back down beside Maya."

"Thanks." Travis did as instructed.

"You were great," Maya said with complete honesty. She chose to leave out what she'd overheard. It wouldn't help him any to know about it.

"Now you're the liar." He playfully swatted her on the nose.

"*That's* what we're looking for!" the loud-whispering executive said. Maya was surprised to find everyone in the room looking right at them.

"Could you two take some shots together?" another executive asked. "Give us some of that chemistry on display in that photo on the Wall."

Maya didn't know what the woman was talking about. When she looked at the picture on the Wall, all she saw was herself and her friends walking out of a club. The rest of it had been manufactured by whoever had written the article. But if "chemistry" would get her the job, she'd do what she could. It wasn't like being intimate with Travis was that hard to do.

Travis stood first and held out a hand to Maya. "You ready for this?"

Maya took his hand. "Guess I can't screw it up any worse."

"There's that positive attitude I love."

They both smiled as they walked in front of Steven and his camera. For the first time, Maya understood what the amateur photographer had said earlier. This smile felt completely genuine.

"Let's start with—oh, that's good." Steven's camera clicked away.

Maya wasn't sure what was good about it. She and Travis were just smiling and looking at each other. They both played into it, smiling wider and suddenly laughing for no reason at all.

"Let's see some smolder," one of the executives suggested.

Maya and Travis let out one last laugh. How were they supposed to be serious with directions like that?

Travis raised his eyebrows in a silent dare. She winked in turn to accept. Their laughter ended. This part was easy. Maya just remembered the first time she'd seen Travis. How he'd come to her rescue when his dad was about to kick her out of school. What he looked like shirtless by the tennis courts later. Before she'd grown suspicious of his intentions. Before her feelings got all confused.

Maya didn't feel the "smolder." What she felt was warm and sweet, not hot and passionate, but it was deeper than friendship. She wanted to cover him in tiny kisses, not high fives and fist bumps.

As the camera continued to click, their hands explored each other's bodies, always aware that they weren't alone, but more intimate than they'd normally be in a public setting. They had to sell that image if they wanted the job. But this was more than just a chance at a gig. This was *something.*

Finally Maya understood what the executive had been talking about in seeing it behind Travis's eyes. She saw something in there now, beyond the hazel with the green flecks. She saw the same thing she knew he saw in hers.

They were never going to be just friends.

Where was Cleo when Maya needed her? Or Renee for that matter?

Travis had been kind enough to give her a ride back to campus so she didn't have to take the bus. The whole drive was awkward and uncomfortable as they both tried to avoid the obvious—there was no better word for it—*chemistry* between them during the shoot. Once they reached the dorm, she practically bolted out of the car to get away from him and tell Cleo everything. But the dorm room was empty and Renee wasn't answering her phone.

They were probably at the dining hall, where it was usually too loud to hear most ringtones. Maya thought about going there, but she didn't need prying eyes watching and eavesdropping ears listening in.

The ring of her own cell phone cut through her tension. Maya was about to yell into it with relief when she stopped herself. It wasn't Cleo's or Renee's name on the caller ID. It was Jordan's.

"Hello?"

"Congratulations," Jordan said by way of greeting. "You booked the campaign."

Maya wasn't sure she'd heard her right. "I'm sorry?"

"You got the job! You're the new face of Esteban's line!"

"Seriously?" Of all the things that had happened to Maya since she got to the Academy, this was the single most impossible to believe.

"It was unanimous. They e-mailed your photos over to Esteban and he agreed immediately. They're going to send me the contract tomorrow."

"Contract?"

"I can look over it for you if you'd like, but I'm going to need a commitment if we're going to go forward on any other jobs. I don't offer freebies to all future clients, but I like you, Maya. If the terms are acceptable, I'll messenger it over along with a formal agreement for us to work together. You can sign the Esteban contract and take some time to look over mine. I'll be in touch."

Jordan ended the call before Maya could even say "Thank you." This seemed to be standard operating procedure with the agent. Get in. Get out. Don't leave time for questions. Maya wasn't crazy about that method, but she couldn't argue with the results. She booked her first ad campaign!

The sudden pounding on her door was much more intense than Renee's had been the night before. "Who is it?"

"Your costar in the Esteban ad campaign!"

Maya flung open the door and threw herself at Travis. They hooted and hollered as they embraced, drawing girls out from their rooms and into the hall. Cell phones came out as people snapped up the moment for posterity, and future postings on the Wall.

"We better get inside." Maya pulled Travis into her room and shut the door before realizing that probably looked a whole lot worse. But she didn't care. She booked her first job. She was going to get paid!

"Jordan called you, too?" Maya asked. Neither of them could sit down. They both had too much energy.

"No. My dad. He's handling my deals until I get an agent. But he told me you got an offer, too. I turned the car around and came right back to celebrate together."

Maya felt horrible. She didn't even think to ask Jordan about Travis. Then again, it wasn't like there had been time to get a word in. "Did you get any details? Jordan hardly told me anything."

"Not at all," Travis said, still beaming. "Those will come with the contract. Maya! We're getting contracts!"

Maya loved to see his reaction to the news. Travis grew up in this world and he was still as excited as she was about it. That made it even better.

"Maya, we're going to be in print ads! Web banners! Billboards!"

In that moment the full scope of this campaign fully hit her. Their pictures would be everywhere. Her friends back home would see them. Nicole would have to look at her face anytime she went to Esteban's boutique.

And Jake would have to see her with Travis everywhere he went.

Chapter 10

"I'm going to get you back, Maya! I'm going to get you back!"

Jake's voice echoed through Maya's sleep-hazy mind as she woke. It wasn't so much a dream as a memory. Jake had sworn that it wasn't over between them. That he wouldn't let it end. But he had.

Jake had completely avoided Maya since the day she almost dropped out of the Academy. If that was how he defined "getting someone back," he had a few things to learn about the English language.

It was what she'd wanted, of course. She'd used that alone time to focus on her game, and the results had been impressive. But Travis ultimately ignored her wishes and moved past the dark time. Jake had sworn he was going to do the opposite of what she'd wanted and then he failed to even do that. There really was no second-guessing him.

Jake stayed on her mind as she got up and ready for her

day. She worried about how he'd react once word got out about the ad campaign. There was no doubt he'd hear about it. That's how things worked in the Reed household. Nails would brag to anyone within the sound of his voice about Travis's new campaign. Maya had to make sure Jake got the news from her.

Finding Jake would be a problem. He wasn't big on sticking to schedules. He was rarely where he was supposed to be. That's why Maya was surprised to find him in the weight room by the football field during his regular time for weight training.

Jake had his back down on the weight bench with arms up, pushing against a barbell. His chest rose and fell with each rep, muscles straining against the pressure.

Maya smiled a greeting at the guy standing over the bench, spotting Jake. He smiled back, but didn't say anything. They both knew better than to distract a person lifting what looked to be Maya's body weight at least.

Once Jake reached the final rep, his spotter helped him guide the barbell onto the hooks above him. With the heavy weapon finally out of his hand, Maya felt it was safe to speak. "Hi," she said.

"Travis isn't here," he replied. His spotter raised his eyebrows and slipped off without saying a word.

"I was looking for you," she said.

"You were?" The smile on Jake's face crushed her a little. It was like nothing had happened between them. Her emotions went right back to when they'd been together.

"Is it that big of a surprise?" she asked.

"A pleasant one," he said as he stood. "I mean . . . to come all the way across campus to search me out. . . . It must be important."

"It is," she said as he moved closer. She could feel the heat rising off his body.

"Is it about . . . us?"

There was hope in his eyes. It killed her to see it there. It made what she'd come to say all that much harder. It also snapped her out of the moment.

Maya took a step back. "It is, but it isn't. It's actually about Travis."

She now felt a different kind of heat coming from him. "Go on."

"Have you heard about the Esteban campaign?"

Jake rolled his eyes. "It's all Dad's been talking about. 'Travis is going places.' 'This is only the beginning for Travis.' So?"

"Did he mention anyone else?"

"No," Jake said. "But he doesn't usually talk about other people when the subject is Travis."

Maya took a deep breath. "I'm in the ad, too. We're both in the ad together."

Jake didn't say anything, but his eyes did.

"I mean . . . not *together,* together. It's not like we went in as a team. It just sort of . . . happened."

Jake shook off the anger in his eyes. He replaced it with a smile like he didn't take any of it seriously. "Yeah, that's how Travis works, isn't it? Things just kind of happen around him."

"You don't really believe your brother set this up, do you?"

Maya asked. Somehow she didn't think they were talking about the ad campaign.

"I don't know anymore," Jake said with a shrug. "Travis used to be my best friend; he had my back even when we were competing against each other. I have no clue who he is now. Not so sure about you either."

Jake sat back on the bench, turning away from Maya. He pulled the pin out of the barbell so he could add some weight. "But, hey, I'm fine if you're dating. I don't get why you'd be with someone you can't trust, but that's your thing."

"We're not dating," she said. "And Travis apologized."

"Not to me." Jake walked away from her, going through the rows of additional weights stacked along the wall. "But it's okay. He doesn't usually apologize when he gets his way these days. I'm used to it."

The thing that bothered Maya most wasn't that Jake was twisting everything; it was that he was so blasé about it. He could have been talking about his class schedule for next semester. He was usually much more emotional about things that mattered to him. Complete apathy was a long way from screaming that he was going to get her back.

"Well, I just wanted to tell you that Travis and I would be working together," Maya said. "Now that you know, I guess there's nothing more to say."

"Thanks for coming by," Jake said, pleasantly enough that it landed like a proverbial punch to the gut. He selected a pair of medium-size weights and brought them back to the bench, making it clear that the conversation wasn't going to distract him from his workout.

Maya turned to leave. Either she'd hurt him so badly that he could barely look at her or he simply didn't care about her anymore. *How could that be true? You don't just forget feelings that intense.* But if Jake didn't want to be friends, she was open to see what her friendship with Travis could become

Of course, there was another option. She was in a school with some of the finest specimens of physical perfection in the world. She didn't need to contain her options to one family. Maybe she could have her friendship with Travis while she played the field. The Academy did have a lot of fields to play on. There were plenty of guys hanging around outside the weight room alone.

Someone grabbed Maya before she could fully explore that idea. She was face-to-frantic-face with Renee. "Maya! Quick, we're in the middle of a conversation. Laugh."

"What?"

"Laugh!"

They both laughed with the most fake-sounding giggles that Maya had ever heard. She was seriously afraid that someone would think they were on drugs.

"What's so funny?" Diego asked.

Suddenly, the insane laughter made sense. At least, as much sense as anything in Renee's boy-crazy world did.

"Oh, it would be too hard to explain," Renee said.

She's right about that, Maya thought.

"So . . . tonight . . . ?" Diego said.

Renee jumped right on it. "I was just talking to Maya about it! She loves the idea."

That didn't sound good.

"You sure?" he asked. "Because we could—"

"I'm sure!" Renee had an edge of panic in her voice. "It's going to be great."

"Okay, then," Diego said. "I've got to get to practice, but I can't wait!"

"Me neither!" Renee said.

The girls watched him run off.

"What's going to be great?" Maya asked.

"You, me, Diego, and Travis," Renee said. "A double date."

"I'm not dating Travis."

"It doesn't have to be a *real* date," Renee said. "Just a group of friends going out together. I mean, it would be a date for me and Diego, but you guys would just be pretending."

"You really think it's a good idea to begin a relationship with a lie?" Maya asked.

"We had such a great time the other night at 360," Renee said. "Everything was so easy. But when it was just the two of us, it was . . . well, I told you how it was. I need you, Maya. Can't you please do this for me?" Renee's eyes pleaded with Maya.

"Okay," Maya said. "But you owe me."

"Oh, Maya!" Renee pulled her friend into a hug. "And I know just how to repay you. I have the most awesome outfit in the world for you to wear. You are going to look hot tonight!"

That wasn't the kind of repayment Maya had in mind. Then again, she liked the idea of looking hot for Travis. Even though they were just friends.

But were they really? Part of her was looking forward to the fake date.

So much for Maya's plan to play the field.

"I felt like a taste of home," Diego said as they stood in front of the Brazilian buffet. Maya had always wanted to try Brazilian food. Her family didn't go out to eat much. When they did, it was usually to a chain restaurant that offered coupons.

"This time, it's on me." Diego turned to Maya and Travis as he opened the door. "I mean, Renee's on me. You two are on your own."

"No problem," Maya said as the scents of the food pleasantly assaulted her senses. "Now that I've got a job, I can afford to eat out once in a while." She didn't actually have the money yet, but that would come soon enough. Her pay for the ad campaign would be more than enough to cover dinners for the month, buy a new wardrobe, and leave her enough extra cash to send some back home. Even after the Academy took its contractually obligated percentage.

The hostess showed them to a table and started handing out menus, but Diego stopped her. "Nope. We're not ordering off the menu. We're doing the buffet. Start bringing out the courses."

The restaurant wasn't like buffets Maya was used to where she and her parents waited in line at serving stations ladling out lukewarm, undercooked food. Diego warned them that this was going to be a different experience entirely.

It started with a gigantic platter with a colorful assortment of veggies covering some lettuce. They called it a salad, but it was so much more.

Maya allowed for a couple of tongs full of vegetables before cutting off the waiter. It looked so delicious, but she wanted to save room for later.

"Don't fill yourselves up too much on the salad," Diego said. "There's plenty more food in the back."

Renee quickly stopped the server after one small serving reached her plate. "Thanks."

"This is delicious," Maya said after her first bite. "It's like an explosion of flavor." She quickly scooped up another, glad that she'd worn her own outfit instead of the one Renee had offered. There was no room for a big meal in anything her friend owned.

"Wait till you get to the meats," Diego said. "The spices they use . . . I hope no one here is a vegetarian."

"If I were, I'd quit for the night," Travis said. "That kitchen smells delicious."

Renee smiled as she took a small bite of her salad. Her face scrunched up noticeably.

"You don't like it?" Diego asked.

Her eyes went wide. "Oh, no. It's delicious! But you said you didn't want us to fill up. It's going to be hard to stop."

But Renee did stop. Maya noticed that she didn't take another bite of the salad. It wasn't unusual. In the time that they'd been friends, Maya never saw Renee once clean her plate.

When the salads were cleared, new plates came out and the fun really began. Waiters carried out more platters with a variety of dishes. They didn't even bother to ask if anyone wanted the food first. They started putting things on the plates until someone stopped them.

Maya didn't want to say no to any of it, which was good because they moved much faster than she did. Renee was the only one who could still see her plate by the time the first wave of waitstaff had passed their table.

Maya caught Diego eyeing Renee's small portions. He was probably spending more on this dinner than any other meal he'd had in his life. Maya wanted to pull Diego aside and explain that Renee simply didn't eat a lot, but there was really no way to do that without making it into something it wasn't.

Renee probably didn't have a full-blown eating disorder, but she did have some messed-up views about food and her body. Of course, if Maya spent all her time in a sport that required her to wear a tight bathing suit in front of hundreds of people, she might have the same issues.

"Isn't this better than that stuffy place we went to the other night?" Diego asked Renee.

She smiled brightly, turning on the charm. "So much better!" Renee punctuated her statement with a small bite of chicken. Diego smiled back at her, but it faltered just a bit when he looked down at her plate again.

"It couldn't have been any stuffier than the place Travis took me to on our first date," Maya said, hoping to direct Diego's attention away from the food.

"It wasn't that bad," Travis said.

Maya just looked at him.

"Okay, it was awful," he agreed. "I was trying too hard."

"Just a bit," Maya said. "He took me to a private drive-in

theater with a movie projected up against a wall and a flood of concession snacks falling out of the glove compartment." Maya recalled the night a bit more fondly than she made it sound. It was actually one of the best dates ever. No one had ever tried that hard for her, misguided as some of it may have been.

"That was *after* the ritzy restaurant I brought her to where she couldn't identify a single thing on the menu," Travis added.

"That's not true!" Maya said. "I recognized the garden salad."

Three of the four people around the table laughed uproariously. Renee smiled, but it was clear she wasn't in on the joke.

"Sounds like that place we went to the other night," Diego said lightly. "I didn't even know what to order."

"I would have helped you," Renee said shyly. The only other time Maya had seen her so soft-spoken was when she once walked in on a phone call between Renee and her parents.

"What are you talking about?" Diego said, laughing. "You didn't eat anything then either."

Three people around the table now got very silent. Diego was the only one who was still smiling. Renee's largely untouched plate suddenly took up a lot of attention.

Slowly, a realization washed over Diego. "Is there something . . . Do you eat?"

"Of course I eat," Renee said. "I just prefer smaller portions. It takes some work to maintain this girlish figure."

"Where I'm from, girls come in all different figures," Diego said. It was a light comment, but Renee clearly took it harder than he'd meant it.

"Some of us have to work to look good," Renee said softly.

"Renee, you're beautiful," Travis said. "Diego, tell her she's beautiful."

"No."

Now *everyone* at the table was silent.

Maya was the first to speak. "Excuse me?"

"She doesn't need me to tell her that," Diego said. "She needs to believe it for herself."

"So . . . you don't think I'm beautiful?" Renee asked.

"I didn't say that," he replied. "I just don't think your beauty has anything to do with the amount of food on your plate." He cut into his steak.

Maya looked to Travis and shrugged. There was something so final about Diego's last comment that she started eating as well. Travis soon followed and even Renee started picking at her food once again. She didn't come close to clearing her plate, but she did eat more than Maya recalled ever seeing her eat before. That was a start.

"Where to now?" Travis asked as the valet brought Renee's car around. Of the two people in the group with cars, hers was the only one with a backseat.

"It's your town," Diego said. "You tell me."

"I don't know. I'm kind of tired." Renee grabbed Maya, pulling her over to the driver's side of the car, whispering, "All is good. I'm ready to go solo with Diego."

"Gotcha," Maya said. She got into the backseat with Travis. "I'm kind of tired, too. Would you all mind if we called it an early evening? I've got a tough practice in the morning."

Maya used the one phrase every Academy student

immediately understood. It ended all discussion without the usual prodding to change her mind.

Renee put the top down on the convertible as they rode back to campus. The noise from the wind gave sufficient privacy to the two couples since their voices barely traveled to the person beside them.

Travis leaned toward Maya so he didn't have to yell. And maybe so he could just be closer. "This was nice," Travis said. "I'm glad we're friends."

Maya rested her hand on top of his on the seat. "I am, too."

Renee dropped Maya off at the dorm with Travis, who had offered to be a gentleman and walk Maya inside. It made no sense whatsoever since Travis had left his car at Renee's villa and Diego lived in the dorm next door. And yet it made complete sense as Renee drove off with Diego.

Since it was after eight, Travis wouldn't be allowed past the lobby. It was clear from the way both of them dragged their feet that they didn't want the night to end. Travis was the first one to acknowledge it.

"You look like you got your second wind," he said as they reached the door.

Maya nodded. There wasn't more to say since she'd been lying about being tired to give Renee some cover. "I'm much more awake than I was leaving the restaurant."

"Great! I want to show you something. It's my favorite part of the campus." Travis took her hand, pulling her around to the side of the dorm.

Maya couldn't imagine what Travis liked about this side of

the campus. The villas and the sports complexes were far better. The scholarship dorms weren't exactly slums, but they were the oldest and least interesting buildings on campus

"Right around here," Travis said as they came to the well.

"Oh," Maya crinkled her nose. Most students in the dorms hated the well because it looked so out of place. The battered old stone well sat under a large concrete archway in the middle of nowhere. Both the well and the archway were gray and crumbling, serving as a stark contrast to the modern Spanish-style villas on the other side of campus.

Travis must have caught her look of confusion. "You know the story about the well, don't you?"

"There's a story?"

"Oh, yeah," Travis said. "Over a hundred years ago the land here was all wilderness. The woods ran up to the property of a railroad magnate, some rich guy who owned pretty much half the state. His daughter fell in love with one of the railroad workers."

"Travis, if this ends with one or both of them dying tragically . . ."

"Just hear me out." Travis sat her down on the edge of the well. "As you already guessed, her father was not happy with the pairing, so he transferred the worker to a whole other part of the country to keep him away from his daughter. And before you say anything, *no*, he didn't refuse to go. This was a different time. He couldn't afford to find other work. He had to do what his boss told him."

"That part, I get," she said.

"Before he left, the workman built this well and the

archway for the girl, as a symbol of his love. He told her to come here to think of him and it would be like they were together.

"At first, the girl couldn't bring herself to visit the well. It hurt too much. But after some time the pain of missing him was worse than the sadness of this reminder. So, she came out here. She sat where you are and sighed his name. A moment later, she was shocked to hear his voice saying hers back.

"The girl looked around, expecting her love to come out from the trees. But he wasn't there. She called out to him, telling him to show himself. This time when he answered, she realized his voice was coming from down in the well. He told her that he'd built an exact replica of the well and the archway where he lived and tied the two together through magic. That way, they could always be together even though they were hundreds of miles apart."

Maya looked down into the well. "You're making that up."

Travis smiled. "I can't take credit for the story. Part of the deal when Dad bought this place was that the well could never be demolished. No one knew why, so people have made up stories over the years to explain it. That one's my favorite."

"So you brought me here to lie to me."

Travis laughed. "No. I brought you here to show you this."

He took her by the hand and moved her over to the archway. The stone arch was concave in the middle. Travis placed a hand gently on her cheek, turning her head so it rested beside the concave part in the center of the stone.

"Stay like that," he said before jogging over to the other side of the well where the arch came down.

"What are you—?"

Travis put a finger up to his lips, shushing her. Then he pointed to the arch, signaling that she should get back into the position he'd left her in. She did as she was told, leaning her ear toward the cold concrete.

"Maya?" Travis's voice whispered from the stone. It sounded like he was leaning right up to her ear.

"Travis!" She looked back. He was all the way on the other side of the arch, a good twenty-five feet away.

"Shhh," his voice whispered. "I can hear you."

"That's incredible," she whispered into the stone. "How did you find this place?"

"My mom showed it to us when we were kids," he said. "Jake and I used to come here to tell each other our secrets. Back before . . ."

He didn't have to finish the sentence. She knew the rest of it: *back before they stopped being close.* Travis and Jake were still friendly, but they weren't close. And that had nothing to do with Maya.

"So, what secret did you bring me here to tell me?" she whispered.

"That I want to be more than friends."

Chapter 11

"Come to the football field." Maya read the text aloud again. "Important."

"It's so vague, yet exciting," Cleo said as they walked down the palm tree–lined pathway.

"You're making fun of me, aren't you?" Maya asked.

"I'm making fun of teenage intrigue," Cleo clarified. "I can't help it if you're the star of that intrigue."

Maya had to laugh. Cleo was right. Things had been pretty intriguing lately.

Days had passed since Travis declared that he wanted more than friendship with Maya. Standing in that archway, she'd wanted to say yes right away, but she told him she wasn't ready to make that commitment. She needed time to think about it. Thankfully both their busy schedules soon got in the way of a follow-up conversation.

Maya's postponed schoolwork started to catch up with

her and practices pulled them away from each other. They spent time at the Academy Exposition meetings together, but coaches, teachers, and the school's publicity team surrounded them from the moment they walked in the door to the time they left. It wasn't the best setting for a private conversation.

Maya still didn't know if she wanted more than friendship with Travis. Part of her did, but not when she thought of Jake. She couldn't imagine telling him she was dating Travis less than a week after she told him that nothing was going on. Then again, considering how indifferent Jake had been about it, that conversation might be a lot easier than she imagined. That bothered her, too. She didn't want Jake to be jealous, but a small part of her wouldn't mind if he was.

"I am a horrible, horrible person."

"Yes. That you are."

"Cleo!"

"Maya, you haven't done anything wrong. You're twisting your emotions in knots to make sure you don't do anything wrong. And for what? One guy who may or may not have schemed against you with your archenemy and another guy who fell into bed with that same enemy point-five seconds after he had the slightest reason to doubt you. If anything, you are a nicer person than either of these guys deserves."

Cleo's point didn't stop Maya from worrying. It did stop her from complaining about her problems, though. Cleo had her own issues. Grant Adams had stepped up his attacks on her and, more importantly, that girl Cleo had met at 360 never even called her back.

Cleo's arm shot out, grabbing Maya and pulling her to the ground. "Duck!"

The girls dropped behind a shrub. Living on a campus full of athletes, the average student was accustomed to swerving out of the way of balls, pucks, javelins, and rogue Frisbees. The past few days had added one more thing for the girls to avoid: cell phone cameras.

"Amateur paparazzo at three o'clock," Cleo explained.

Maya peeked over the shrub in time to see the frustrated girl put away her phone and stomp off in the opposite direction. "I don't get it. We weren't even doing anything."

"Maya, you're about to walk onto the football field, where the two guys you've been linked to on the Wall are practicing. And I'm . . . well, I'm me!"

Cleo was looking particularly Cleo that afternoon in an oversized vintage Debbie Harry T-shirt that revealed half her sports bra, jeans with skulls painted on the back pockets, and a pair of kick-ass boots. A shot of her in that outfit would give Grant Adams plenty to write about in his next blog post.

Cleo had been trying to dig up all the dirt she could find on the guy, but it was useless. No one knew anything about him beyond his blog.

"All clear." Maya brushed the grass from her jeans as she got off the ground.

Cleo picked a leaf out of her friend's hair. "This is annoying."

"Down!" Maya yelled through clenched teeth.

They both dropped. It was becoming second nature.

"Beyond annoying," Cleo said. "That thing on the Wall was a week ago."

Maya took out her phone. She was afraid to look, but she knew there would be an answer online. "Nothing new on the Wall."

"Thank heaven for small favors." Cleo took the phone from her friend, typing on the little keypad on the screen. "Oh."

"Oh, what?"

"Grant Adams put some kind of bounty on my head," Cleo said as she stood. When she handed the phone back to Maya, the screen was blank.

Maya wanted to look, but she knew Cleo would kill her if she did. "Cleo!"

Cleo dropped to the ground again out of habit.

"No," Maya said. "I mean, tell me what you're talking about!"

Cleo let out an exaggerated sigh as she got back up. "Nothing big. He posted a photo contest. The person who gets a picture of me in the craziest outfit wins an online interview from Grant."

"What kind of prize is that?"

"Only the best prize ever." Cleo continued walking toward the football field. "He knows where I go to school. Every student in this place would kill for that kind of exposure. Not just the golfers."

Maya still had the Esteban scarf she'd borrowed from Renee. She took it from around her neck and opened it up to its full size. "Here, wrap yourself in this."

Cleo held out a hand, but stopped herself before she took the scarf. "No. I'm not going to let some stuffy old dude win. If I'm going to be me, I'm going to be me."

Cleo took her own cell phone out of the pocket of her jeans and held the camera out at arm's length, lining her body up in the screen.

Maya grabbed the phone. "What are you doing?"

"I'm giving Grant a good shot of me," she replied. "Or maybe I should wait. I have *much* better things in my closet. I could probably put something together that gives him a heart attack."

"You can't play his game," Maya said.

"Why not?"

"Well, for one thing, do you want him to have your e-mail address or phone number when you send the picture?"

"Good point. Besides, what does it matter? I think he's got me pretty covered." Cleo tipped her head to the side as she spoke.

Maya followed the tilt of Cleo's head to see a guy with a camera phone pointed at them. It didn't end there. About a half-dozen cell phones were aimed in their direction. Grant Adams's photo contest was bad enough, but the fact that their classmates would sell out one of their own for a little free publicity really upset Maya.

Cleo was right. There was nothing they could do about it, short of wrapping Cleo in a blanket as she walked from class to class. That wasn't the answer to anything. Although Maya was tempted to drape that Esteban scarf over her own head so she didn't appear on any more blogs.

Maya was surprised to see Renee waiting for them outside the football field. "It's about time you two got here," Renee said. "What took you so long?"

"We had to stop and pose for a dozen photos on the way," Cleo replied.

"And we didn't know you were waiting," Maya added. "What are you doing here?"

"Cleo told me about the text," Renee said. "Sounded intriguing."

Maya shot a glare at her friend. "Thanks, Cleo."

Cleo smiled brightly. "No problem!"

Renee grabbed Maya's arm and pulled her toward the field. "Are we sitting in the spot reserved for girlfriends today?"

"No!" Maya said. That was the last thing she needed. She'd done that before and once was enough. "No girlfriend spot. We're sitting in the bleachers. The very top of the bleachers. Behind a pillar, if possible."

Renee shook her head. "You're no fun."

"Not as fun as Cleo, apparently," Maya said as a few more camera clicks followed them to the stands. The word was out. Everyone wanted a shot of Cleo, which was just silly at this point. A couple hundred photos of Cleo in the same outfit weren't going to win anything.

"Oh, shut up," Cleo said.

Heads continued to turn as the three girls made their way up to the top of the bleachers. Maya wanted to credit the interest to Cleo, but she knew some of it was for her as well. No matter where she sat, Maya wasn't fooling anyone. They knew she was there to see one of the Reed brothers. They all wanted to know which one.

Both brothers looked good. Travis was in control as quarterback, guiding his teammates down the field. He was a study of perfection and control. Maya had learned enough about football to hold her own in a conversation, and even she was blown away by how Travis managed his plays.

Jake was the real surprise, though. His game was very un-Jake-like. And that was a good thing.

The first time Maya came by to watch a practice, Jake incited a lawsuit with his aggressive play and a move that injured one of his classmates. That Jake wasn't on the field. Jake 2.0 played with far more control than she'd seen in him before. He looked more like his brother than ever.

Maya didn't have a chance to see too much since the coach called the scrimmage to an end shortly after she arrived. Maya planned to stay on the bleachers and wait for Travis to come out of the locker room and tell her what he needed to say. By then, most of the spectators would be gone, taking their camera phones with them. Travis threw a major wrench into that plan when he came to the sideline and waved his arms at her like she was a million miles away.

She only wished she were a million miles away at that moment.

"I think Travis has seen you," Cleo said. "But I could be wrong."

Maya reluctantly stood. If she ignored him, that would only make it worse.

Cleo and Renee stood along with her.

"Stop!" Maya said. "Sit! Stay!"

The girls did as they were told. Maya had enough of an audience. She didn't need her friends along when Travis said what he wanted to say to her.

Heads turned again as she made the long walk down the bleachers. Her supposedly invisible seat in the back row meant she had even farther to walk while everyone stared. She could feel the eyes of the dozens of students following her every step. She focused on Travis's eyes instead. That, and the fact that Jake's eyes had disappeared into the locker room without even a backward glance.

"I'd give you a hug, but I'm kind of sweaty," Travis said once she was closer.

"I see that." Maya saw a lot of him in his tight muscle shirt.

"You got my text?"

Maya thought that was pretty obvious. Unless he was hoping she'd stopped by to see him on a whim. Suddenly, she felt bad about not doing that sooner. "Yeah."

Travis's eyes now looked uncertain. "Something huge has happened."

"Huge good or huge bad?"

"Huge awesome," Travis replied. "I booked a guest spot on *The Hype*."

"*The Hype*?" she asked. "On SNC? *That Hype*?"

Travis's lips broke into the winning grin that was so much like his dad's. The only difference was that Travis's smile didn't reach his eyes. He was happy, but wary. "Yes. *That Hype.*"

"Travis, that *is* awesome!" Maya wrapped him in a congratulatory hug. His after-practice glow didn't matter. *The Hype* was one of the Sports News Channel's most popular shows. For an amateur—a *high school student*—to appear as a guest was the hugest of the huge. Which is why Maya was nervous that she couldn't feel him hugging her back.

"What is it?"

"They're flying me to New York to shoot the segment."

"Okay."

"On . . . Friday."

"Oh." The same day as their photo shoot for Esteban's sportswear line.

"Dad's trying to get the shoot moved," he quickly said. "He's working every angle. If anyone can get it switched, it would be him."

Maya couldn't help but notice that Nails wasn't working on getting Travis's appearance on *The Hype* moved, considering the Esteban ad had come first.

"And if he can't?" Maya asked.

"I made a commitment to the Esteban campaign," Travis said. "And to you."

"To me?"

"I know how important this shoot is," he said. "I don't want to risk messing it up for you . . . money being tight and all."

Was he only doing the shoot for Maya? Of course an appearance on *The Hype* was more important to his career than some fashion shoot. College recruiters and NFL coaches watched the Sports News Channel. They didn't tend to be impressed by fashion ads when making their player selections.

Considering how many of their classmates were willing to sell out Cleo for an interview with a golf blogger, most of them would probably commit murder to appear on *The Hype*.

"Travis," she said, "you have to go on *The Hype.* You can't miss that kind of opportunity for an ad campaign."

"I will in a second," he said. "If you want me to."

If you want me to? Would he really blow off the opportunity for her? That was nice, but how could he put that on her?

Just because Travis pulled out of the shoot didn't mean that it would be canceled. Or that Maya would be out as well. They were two different people. But she couldn't shake the feeling that they'd been hired as a couple, whether or not they actually were a couple at the time. Or now even. They really did have to have that conversation at some point.

If she stood in the way of Travis's opportunity for that press, they might never have the chance to be a couple again. Nails would see to that. He could make life very difficult for Maya if he felt she was standing in the way of his son's success.

There really wasn't a decision to make, when she thought about it. All she could do was go along, and hope that everything worked out.

"Of course you should do it," she said. "You'd be an idiot not to."

And yet, in that moment, Maya was the one who felt like the fool.

It didn't help that when she turned to the bleachers, she saw that the stands were still full of people who'd stuck around to watch the postgame show.

Chapter 12

"I'm on it." That was how Jordan answered the phone. No wasting time with pleasantries. She cut right to the chase. *"I've already got a couple calls in to the agency. Sit tight. I'll get back to you."*

And she was gone.

That was the sum total of the conversation Maya had had with Jordan two days ago. There was no hand-holding, no reassurances that Maya still had the job, no indications that there was any backup plan at all if one of them dropped out of the shoot as Travis had.

Maya hadn't heard anything from Jordan or Travis and the shoot was the next day. At least, she hoped it was still the next day.

She wanted to call Jordan back. She wanted to pester the agent until she heard something. But Maya had that unsigned agreement in front of her. She figured she didn't have any right to expect the agent to make her a priority if Maya couldn't even decide if she wanted Jordan to represent her.

"Here we go again," Cleo said from her computer.

Maya was afraid to ask. "Grant Adams?"

"Yep."

"Did he find a winner for the worst outfit?"

"Not yet," Cleo said. "This is worse than a picture. He's going after me on something new. He's got a whole write-up here on how I've completely turned my back on my heritage."

"WHAT?!"

Maya was off her bed and leaning over Cleo's shoulder. Grant Adams really did a number on her this time. It was one thing to make fun of Cleo's clothes. She dressed like she didn't care what other people thought, so it was only natural that people felt it was their duty to tell her what they thought. But this messed with her family.

The article went to great lengths to examine how "Americanized" Cleo had become, from her clothes, to her friends, to the fact that she didn't go by her real name, Li Sun, anymore. The blog was filled with pictures of her on campus and out on the town doing things a typical teen would do with friends. None of it was scandalous until Grant Adams put his small-minded spin on every image. Suddenly a picture of her eating a hot dog opened up a discourse on national pride.

Even worse, the photos came from all over. Their classmates had been busy this week invading Cleo's privacy. Maya was going to have to talk to Travis about getting his father to make some kind of ban on cell-phone photos around the school. No one should be put through this kind of cyber-stalking.

Maya expected Cleo to scream and throw things, promising revenge. It was much scarier that she got very, very quiet. It broke Maya's heart to see a tear drop from her friend's eye. Cleo didn't get sad. She got angry. Very angry.

Maya rested a hand on Cleo's shoulder. "Are you okay?"

"No," Cleo said. "But I'm going to do something about it. I just don't know what. Yet."

Maya hated to leave Cleo, but there wasn't anything more she could do. They'd spent an hour discussing ways to get back at Grant Adams, but came up with nothing. When the text from Travis came through telling Maya that he couldn't move the shoot, Cleo insisted that Maya go talk to him and see what was up.

"I'm so sorry," Travis said the moment Maya walked into Ground Rules, the coffee shop halfway between the football field and the dorms. Travis had slipped out of practice to talk to her, which was uncharacteristic of him. He had to meet somewhere he could get back before he was missed.

He handed her an iced mocha latte with extra whipped cream and chocolate sauce. It had to be over five hundred calories. Maya took the excessive sugar as an added apology.

"Thanks," she said. "And it's okay."

It wasn't completely "okay," though. What would happen with the shoot? Did they still want her? How was she supposed to do this without Travis?

"Maya, you don't have to be so understanding," Travis

said. "You have every right to be upset with me for bailing on you."

Maya was upset, but not with Travis. She was worried about what it meant for her. "You made a business decision. It's the kind of thing we're going to have to do. I can't take it personally."

"I don't deserve a friend like you."

Maya smiled. "Well, I won't argue with *that*."

Their laughter broke the tension, until they both homed in on that word: "friend." They still hadn't discussed what Travis had whispered at the old well.

Travis looked like he was about to bring it up just as Maya's phone rang. She quickly checked the screen and saw a now familiar number.

"It's Jordan," she said. "I'm sorry. I have to take this."

Maya left her latte on the table and went outside before answering the call. She didn't want everyone in the coffee shop to eavesdrop on her conversation. She especially didn't want to make Travis listen to it. If Jordan had bad news, Maya didn't have the acting chops to pretend everything was fine in front of Travis.

Maya answered the phone as she walked through the patio. She'd hoped for a more secluded spot, but she had to get the call before it rolled over to voice mail. "Hello?"

"You're still in for now," Jordan said by way of greeting.

Maya froze in place on the patio. That didn't sound good. "For now?"

"They want to test you with some more guys," Jordan said. "See if you can re-create that spark."

"And if I can't?"

"Then they'll have to go with someone else."

Jordan wasn't one to sugarcoat things. Maya appreciated that, but she didn't entirely like it. There was nothing wrong with a little bit of coddling. But that was a discussion for another time. The ad agency people wanted her back at their offices. Immediately.

Flashbacks of Maya's movie audition invaded her thoughts as the elevator doors opened to the lobby of the Creative Core. Those memories were joined by her more recent recollections of her audition for the ad campaign. Could she find chemistry with a total stranger?

There was no waiting this time. Steven bolted from the audition room moments after she stepped out of the elevator. Either they had cameras trained on the lobby or, more likely, the receptionist hit the intercom the moment Maya was in sight.

"Maya, thank you so much for coming." He shook her hand, then kept holding it as he guided her through the lobby. His frantic manner didn't help calm Maya's nerves any as he walked her past a half-dozen guys of various sizes and shapes toward the audition room. The one thing the guys had in common was that they were all hot. Incredibly hot.

"I'm happy to be here," she said. As if she had a choice. Jordan made the situation clear. They could still go with someone else.

Steven escorted her into the room where the same executives sat in the same spots they had when she'd been there a week earlier. It was like they had assigned seating.

"Maya, thank you so much for coming back in," the executive in the middle said. "Sorry to make you go through this process again, but we need to be sure the chemistry is right before we commit. This is going to be a major campaign."

"No, I totally understand," Maya said. She especially understood that she wasn't a lock for the campaign. These new guys may have been coming in to test with her, but she was going to have to impress her critics all over again.

"Let's get started," the chief executive said.

"Sounds good," Maya agreed with a big smile to show them she was ready for anything.

Steven brought in the first guy. Maya didn't want to make assumptions, but she guessed he played basketball because of his size. Maya was pretty tall herself, but this guy dwarfed her by at least a foot. Before he even reached her, she knew it wasn't going to work, but she kept her smile on and gave it her best attempt.

She was about to introduce herself when Steven started giving direction. "Can you just wrap an arm around her, real quick?"

"Sure." The guy did what he was told. Maya's head only came up to his chest.

Steven didn't even raise his camera. He looked over a shoulder. The executive in the middle seat gave a slight shake of his head. And the guy was excused before Maya had the chance to say hello.

The next guy was more Maya's height and she did have a chance to introduce herself as they took some pictures together. His name was Jasper, and he had exactly the kind of smolder

Steven asked for. Unfortunately, every time he smoldered in Maya's direction, she broke out in giggles.

"I'm so sorry," she said for the fifth time. What he was doing looked great, but it just felt so fake. To Maya, there was nothing behind his eyes, but she didn't hear any of the executives make that comment like they had with Travis.

"Okay, thanks," Steven said, and the guys rotated again.

Maya quickly went through the half-dozen guys feeling less and less confident with each one. It was not going well at all.

The last guy, Grayson, was so good that Maya felt like she was losing the job with each new pose. She came off like a complete amateur next to him, which she was. They'd said they wanted amateurs for the shoot, but this guy knew his way around a camera. He looked familiar, too. Maybe she'd seen him around school.

"It's okay, Maya," Grayson whispered into her ear as he held her from behind. "Just relax your body. Let me hold you up. I promise I'll keep you in a position that maximizes your look."

Maya tried to relax and let him take control, but she didn't understand how this amateur knew what kind of control to take. Or how to "maximize her look." She couldn't imagine many of her classmates using that phrase.

Suddenly Maya realized why Grayson looked so familiar. As they shifted poses to a face-to-face embrace, Maya struck up a whispered conversation. "Grayson, are you the Tactics guy?"

Grayson's smile brightened. "You recognized me, huh? I

got a lot of work out of that campaign. Get stopped on the street a lot, too."

"It's good work," Maya said as she struggled to find a comfortable pose. Grayson wasn't an athlete. He was the guy in the Tactics body spray ads. He was practically famous for that ad campaign.

They'd paired Maya with professionals. No wonder she felt like even more of an amateur than she had before.

Steven put down his camera. "Okay, Grayson. Thanks! We're done." He looked down at his cell phone, then whispered something to the executives.

Maya said good-bye to Grayson and hung around to see what they wanted next from her. It wasn't much.

"Thank you as well, Maya," the head executive said as Steven hurried out of the room. She wondered if he was running after Grayson to tell him he'd booked the job.

"Happy to do it," Maya said. She wasn't sure if she'd already said that back when they started. She'd been posing for over an hour and her mind was filled with awkward body positions and inappropriate laughter. She had managed to screw this audition up without any help from Nicole King.

"We'll let your agent know once we've decided on the direction we plan to take," he said.

Maya felt like she should say something more. Maybe offer to take modeling classes if there was such a thing. But she didn't want to look like she was begging.

The lobby was empty, except for the receptionist. It sounded like she was on a personal call. She was talking about her plans for the weekend and the model she'd just made a date with. Maya wondered if she meant Grayson.

The woman looked up at Maya questioningly, though she didn't stop talking on the phone.

Maya mouthed: "Is Steven around? I wanted to thank him."

The receptionist jerked her head to the right, which Maya took as the general direction his desk was in. Growing up the daughter of a gardener, Maya knew that thanking the "little people" was the best way to be remembered by the bigwigs.

Steven was easy to find. He had a small outer office with a big glass window at the edge of a cubicle farm. Maya was about to enter when she saw a dark-haired girl in his guest chair. Nicole.

Maya hid behind a giant potted fern by the door as she listened in.

"They should be wrapping up in a minute," he said. "I'm sure Mr. Williams would love to meet you."

"Thanks," Nicole said. "I'm so sorry to just show up like this, but I heard a rumor that you were looking for someone and, well, Esteban and I do have a history. He designed the dress I wore to prom last year."

"Actually, I did know that," Steven said. "Saw the pictures in *US Weekly.* The only reason we didn't request you in the first place was they were looking for someone less famous. An unknown. But I think that might be changing."

"Well, if you want a nobody, you should definitely go with Maya Hart," Nicole said. "But if you're looking for someone who comes with a little something extra, well . . ." She let the words trail off to allow him to fill in the blanks.

Maya wanted to fill in some blanks as well.

"I'll go see what's keeping them," he said.

Maya dropped back farther behind the fern as Steven passed her. She considered slipping out quietly, but she wanted Nicole to know that she was onto her this time. "Hello, Nicole."

"Maya! So nice to see you." If Nicole was surprised that she'd been caught, she didn't show it.

"Trying to take another job from me?"

"Oh, Maya," she said, "I don't take things. People just give them to me when they see what I have to offer."

Maya noticed that Nicole was holding her arm. "How's the wrist?"

Nicole smiled with clenched teeth. "Fine."

"Glad to hear it," Maya said. "Guess I'll see you back at school."

"Yes," Nicole said. "You will."

Maya wasn't sure what she'd accomplished with that little exchange, but it felt good to confirm that she knew something Nicole didn't want her to know. Not that it mattered. Maya wasn't going to do anything about it. And even if she did, it wouldn't affect the ad campaign. Nicole could do those poses in her sleep, whether her wrist was injured or not.

Maya had done all that she could about the campaign. Now she just had to wait for Jordan to call.

Assuming that Jordan was still on her side.

Chapter 13

Maya read the agreement Jordan had sent over. It was probably the twentieth time she'd read the document and she still couldn't decide what to do about it. She'd gone over the agreement with Travis. She'd asked one of her coaches to look at it. She even sent a copy to her dad, even though he was just as lost as she was when it came to the legalese. Whoever Maya signed with would have major control over her career and her life. She so wasn't ready for this kind of decision.

It was getting late, but Maya couldn't go to bed without knowing if she had class in the morning or a photo shoot. After the first audition, Jordan called with the news by the time she'd gotten back to her dorm. But this time, nothing. Jordan hadn't returned any of her calls. It was not good a sign.

Suddenly, Maya's cell phone hovered in front of her eyes.

"Call her," Cleo said, shaking the phone.

Maya pushed it away. "I've called her. Multiple times."

Cleo pushed the phone back. “Call her again. You said yourself this is a trial period. She’s stopped trying. You don’t have to look at that contract anymore. She picked Nicole over you. What more is there to think about?”

“You’re right.” Maya took the phone from Cleo and tapped Jordan’s name. If she didn’t answer, Maya would leave a message thanking the agent for her time, but telling her she was taking her business someplace else. She started rehearsing the voice mail in her head as the phone rang.

“Sorry I’ve been out of touch lately, but I’ve been working my magic to keep you on the campaign.”

Maya’s eyes went wide, along with Cleo’s. Jordan’s voice was loud enough that her side of the conversation filled the small dorm room even without speakerphone.

“I still have the job?” Maya asked. The short speech she’d prepared for Jordan’s voice mail went right out of her head.

“You’ve still got the job,” Jordan confirmed. “It was touch and go there for a bit. They considered going the professional model route—”

“You mean the Nicole King route,” Cleo added.

“What was that?” Jordan asked. Apparently Cleo’s voice carried as well.

Maya shot Cleo a warning glare. “Nothing.”

“Maya? Is there something I should know?”

Maya sighed. “I saw Nicole at the agency. I know you sent her.”

“Sent Nicole?” Jordan said. “Maya, I did not send Nicole anywhere. If she was there, she did that on her own. Which is something she does quite often. I'm sorry if you got caught up in it, but it's nothing to concern yourself with."

The words were apologetic, but Jordan's voice was quite matter-of-fact, as if this kind of thing happened and Maya should just get over it. *After all*, as Jordan had said, *this is business, not high school.*

Maya was still suspicious. "How did she even find out about it?"

Jordan laughed. "Maya, everybody knows about it. You can't keep a secret in this industry. None of that matters, because you're back in the campaign. We found a perfect replacement for Travis with a fresh face and equally recognizable name."

Maya knew exactly where this conversation was going.

Jordan confirmed her suspicions with one little word: "Jake."

The shade of the large umbrella failed to keep Maya cool. It was an unseasonably warm day, which for Florida meant extremely hot and humid. Maya would have been fine if she were just wearing Esteban's purple-and-gray short-sleeve bodysuit and matching canvas shorts. The fabrics were light and breathable. But the photo shoot was outdoors and everyone was afraid that someone might sneak a picture of the clothes and leak it to the press. Maya and Jake had to wear long overcoats to cover up while they waited for the production to finish prepping.

Even though the NFL stadium that provided their setting was on complete lockdown, it didn't mean anything to the hyper-security-conscious ad agency. Thankfully Steven had sent over some fans to keep Maya from sweating off her professionally applied makeup.

Jake had his own umbrella of shade less than ten feet away, but it might as well have been a million miles. He'd barely looked at her since he arrived. So much for Renee's crazy suggestion that he only agreed to shoot the ad because he wanted to be closer to Maya.

"We'll be ready in five," Steven told her. It was the sixth time he'd given her a five-minute warning. She didn't bother taking off the coat as she had the first two times. She'd just have to put it back on again with the next delay.

"No!" the photographer, Charles Zin, yelled. "The sun is in the wrong position. This is not going to work at all!"

Maya peeked out from under the umbrella. She didn't know what position he wanted the sun to be in. It shined down on the field with maximum efficiency. There was hardly a shadow for the rest of the crew to hide in to keep cool. The photographer had complained about the sun in the sky, the coloring of the Astroturf beneath their feet, and everything in between.

Maya's phone buzzed in the pocket of her overcoat. Travis had sent her a message: Break a leg! Preferably Jake's.

Maya wrote back: lol! u 2!

It was nice to know she was on his mind even though he had a bunch of other things to think about. Not only was his appearance on *The Hype* scheduled for the same day as the shoot, but it was at the same time, too. He went on in a half hour. Maya wasn't even sure she'd be shooting by then. There was no way she'd be able to catch it. But that's what DVRs were for.

Maya spent the next few minutes texting with Travis before he had to go to set. By the time she was done, she got another five-minute warning from Steven.

"You keep saying that," Maya said lightly.

"This time I actually believe it," he replied. "Esteban has arrived."

Maya didn't know how she'd missed him. The famous clothing designer had come onto the field in a pink-and-white zebra-striped suit and an entourage of people dressed entirely in black. They sat under a red sequined tent the photographer had spent the first half hour of the day screaming about because of the light reflection. The production assistant had moved the tent back to the fifty yard line, but now Esteban's people were having a fit about being so far from the action in the end zone. These next five minutes were probably going to take a while, no matter what Steven said.

Everyone on the crew tended to Esteban and the photographer, leaving Maya and Jake all alone on the side of the field. It finally got to the point of beyond awkward that they were sitting right next to each other without speaking. Maya figured it was time to be the bigger person. She got up from her folding chair and slipped under Jake's umbrella.

"Travis is about to go on," she said.

"I know," Jake said without looking at her.

At this point, Maya had had enough. "Okay, seriously, Jake? What is this about?"

He finally looked at her, genuinely confused. "What is what about? You said you didn't want be together anymore. I'm giving you your space."

"Space is one thing," she said. "Totally ignoring me is another."

Jake stood. "You may have noticed that I'm not good at doing things halfway. I'm either all in or all out. You didn't want me in, so I'm out. Obviously, some people don't have that problem."

"This isn't about Travis," she said.

"I never said it was. I was talking about you."

"We're ready to go," Steven jumped in. "Better move fast before the next major cataclysm occurs, like someone finds out there's no sushi on the snack table."

Jake threw off his overcoat and took the field, leaving Maya behind. How she'd get through this shoot with someone who obviously hated her was a mystery.

Three wardrobe changes in, the shoot was just as awkward as it had been when they started. The shots in the end zone were good as long as Maya and Jake didn't have to look at each other. The ones in the bleachers quickly became single poses since Zin, the photographer, claimed he was getting nothing from his subjects when they were together.

The crew had moved onto the press box for the final setup of the day. On the bright side, the press box was shaded and air-conditioned. Unfortunately, this part of the plan called for the most intimate poses of the shoot. If the earlier scenes were any indication, this would not go well.

Maya wore the signature design for the line. Esteban had created a dress that would look good on the court and, with a few minor alterations, out on the town. It was the most comfortable outfit Maya had ever been in. She couldn't imagine an occasion where she would ever go from the court to a club in the same clothing, but sometimes fashion was more about form than function. This was one of those times.

"I get to take this home with me, right?" Maya joked to Steven.

"No," he replied, stern-faced. "If that dress gets out, you'd be killed, I'd be fired, and Esteban would probably need to be institutionalized."

Maya shrunk back. "I was kidding."

Steven remained straight-faced. "I wasn't."

Something behind Maya distracted Steven. He was no longer looking at her. She turned to see what he was gawking at and her own jaw dropped.

Jake wore a brown linen sport jacket over a white, skin-tight tank top made from some kind of material that shimmered without too much shine. His pants hugged the muscles of his legs, but still gave him room to move. It was sporty, yet casually professional at the same time. Maya could see him on the sidelines or in the boardroom. Jake looked so mature in the outfit that she could easily imagine him taking over the Academy one day, even though she knew it would never happen.

Zin pulled Maya and Jake together. "We've sold the sport, now it's time to sell the passion. You two, up on the desk."

"What?" Maya asked.

"The desk?" Jake said.

"She's a pretty girl," the photographer said in the most condescending way he could. "I'm sure you can figure out what to do, Reed."

"My name is Jake," he replied. "Reed is my dad."

Maya could have sworn she heard him say "And my brother" under his breath. It figured that the "Reed boys" would want to make their names for themselves. And it was just like Jake to be the one to correct people about it while Travis silently let others call him what they wanted.

Zin patted his hand like he was calling for a pair of puppies to jump up on the table. "On the desk, please."

Maya didn't exactly know what he was going for with the shoot, but the atmosphere suddenly felt much less sporting. On the field and in the stands, he'd posed them in action shots that accentuated the clothes while focusing on sports. This was more personal and, in Maya's mind, kind of tacky. Since she didn't want to cause a problem, she started to climb onto the table.

"No," Zin said. "Jake on the table. I want Maya to be the aggressor."

Jake smiled for the first time all day. "This is going to be fun."

Maya gave him a swat on the arm. "Dream on."

Jake slid onto the desk and waited for further instruction. His smile had turned to a smirk that Maya alternately wanted to smack off his face . . . or kiss.

Where did that *come from?*

They both looked at the photographer.

Zin raised an eyebrow. "Do you really need me to tell you what to do?"

Jake shrugged, and leaned back on the table next to the glass window overlooking the field. He stayed up on his elbows so Maya wouldn't have to bend so far to reach him. From where Maya stood, she could tell that the image of them together beside the glass with the field below them was going to be powerful. So long as she didn't screw it up.

Maya leaned over Jake with her body closer to his than she'd been in a while. This time, he couldn't ignore her; he couldn't look away.

Maya was semi-aware of the camera clicking in the background, but it was the last thing on her mind. All she could think of was Jake. She breathed in the familiar sandalwood scent of his cologne, felt his heart beat through his muscular chest. "Lose the jacket, Jake," Zin whispered.

Jake leaned forward, starting to do what he was told, but Maya stopped him. She grabbed the jacket material in her hand and heard an audible gasp from Esteban. It didn't matter if the designer was upset that she crinkled the fabric, the absolute stillness from the rest of the room told her it worked.

Maya pulled the jacket off Jake. He went along, moving as she directed him, leaving her in control.

She dropped the jacket to the floor, eliciting another gasp from the designer as it crumpled to the ground. Maya kicked it out of the frame as she lifted a leg to the table. The material of the skirt moved with her body, protecting her modesty as her moves became almost completely indecent in front of a room full of strangers.

All she saw was Jake.

All he saw was Maya.

So many sense memories filled her from their brief relationship, it was like they were transported back in time. They weren't in the press box of a football stadium. They were on the couch in his place, the first time they'd kissed.

Being near Jake—so close to him—it all came back.

"Perfect," the photographer whispered.

Their faces were inches apart. There was only one thing left. One thing Maya knew she couldn't do. One thing she couldn't ignore.

She leaned in closer. Her lips brushed against his.

The scene on the couch playing in her mind jump-cut to another image: Nicole in Jake's T-shirt; Jake, drunk and in bed. The afternoon Maya's heart had been broken.

Maya's foot dropped to the floor of the press box as she broke away from Jake. The image was so jarring that she nearly lost control.

"I'm sorry," she said with tears fighting to escape. "I'm sorry."

Maya fled the room, leaving Jake and everyone else behind.

Chapter 14

"It was awful." Maya bit into a non-vegan Vanilla Dream cupcake. She meant her abrupt exit from the photo shoot. The cupcake was actually quite tasty.

"It's never as bad as you think," Renee assured her while picking at her cupcake with her finger.

"Sometimes it's worse," Cleo added through her own mouthful of cupcake.

Maya had stopped off at the Cupcakery on the way back from the shoot. She figured she'd feel less horrible about drowning her sorrows in sugary snacks if she brought some for her friends.

"I *bolted*," Maya said. "Ran out in the middle of the shoot. It was embarrassing and totally unprofessional."

"And yet you still took the time to change out of that fabulous Esteban original and return it to its security vault," Renee reminded her as she took a small bite from her cupcake. "Totally professional."

"I can't imagine what Jake thinks," Maya said. "I thought I'd moved past him."

Cleo finished the last bit of her cupcake. "You probably did. We all backslide. Just when I think I'm over that girl from the club blowing me off, the phone rings and I get all hopeful again. And I don't even know her last name! Your thing with Jake was way more intense."

"It *was* intense," Maya agreed. "I think it still is."

Renee dropped her cupcake in the trash can beside Cleo's bed. She'd taken three bites out of it, which was more than Maya had expected. "Look, Maya, I don't mean to be cold, but you have to prioritize. Worry about Jake later. You have to find out about the shoot. How much was left on the schedule?"

Maya wiped a stray tear with her napkin. "We were on the last outfits. That's probably the only reason that photographer didn't come into the dressing room and carry me back into the press box."

"That's good," Renee said. "No harm, no foul. I'm sure the campaign is fine."

On cue, Maya's cell phone vibrated. Jordan's name came up on the screen. Maya held it out for her friends to see. "I don't want to answer it."

Cleo grabbed the phone. "Good. She kept you waiting long enough before the shoot. Maybe you should keep her waiting, too."

Renee pulled the phone from Cleo's hand and gave it back to Maya. "Now you *are* being unprofessional. You need to find out what's going on. Don't let some guy make you less than you are."

Cleo raised an eyebrow. "That was profound."

"Of course it was," Renee said. "I make guys feel that way all the time."

Maya smiled as she answered Jordan's call.

As usual, Jordan got right to the point. "Maya, they loved you."

"They did? But I ran out of the shoot."

"Nobody said anything about that," Jordan replied. "They were too busy raving about the photos. Guess I was right about your chemistry with those Reed brothers." Maya had to wonder just how much Jordan knew about her personal life.

"Get some rest this weekend," Jordan suggested, "and we can sit down next week to start planning for your future." And with that, the call was over.

The last thing Maya wanted to worry about was her future. She couldn't even figure out what to do in the present.

Cleo's voice took the place of Maya's alarm clock. "Here we go again."

"What now?" Maya had a sense of déjà vu as she woke Saturday morning. She'd been so exhausted by the emotional upheaval of the day before—combined with a sugar crash from the cupcake—that she fell asleep way earlier than normal.

Cleo had a bright, big, and incredibly fake smile plastered on her face. "Guess who's back on the Wall?"

"Oh, Cleo! I'm so sorry."

"Wrong again! It's you!"

"Ugh. Now I really am sorry." Maya pulled her pillow out

from under her head and held it over her face. She did not want to begin her day like this.

Cleo pulled against the pillow, but Maya held tight. "You can't hide under that pillow. You're far too tall."

Maya released the pillow so abruptly that it slipped out of Cleo's hand and hit the ceiling before falling back to the floor. Cleo slid her laptop onto the bed. The screen was filled by an extreme close-up of Maya as she was about to go in for a kiss with Jake.

Maya bolted upright. "The photos leaked from the shoot?"

The picture had to be from the half second before she ran out of the room. The headline above it read: "Brotherly Love."

The title summarized the article succinctly. The story was about how Maya played Travis and Jake off each other. Not only did the article include those shots of Maya coming out of 360, but it also had the picture of her with Jake at Sour weeks ago. The story quoted an anonymous friend saying that Maya couldn't make her mind up between the brothers.

"Anonymous friend?" Maya asked.

"Gee, I wonder?" Cleo said

There was no real question. Nicole's manicured fingerprints were all over it.

"This is awful," Maya said.

Cleo took the laptop back. "I'm surprised your phone hasn't been blowing up all morning. This story was posted an hour ago."

Maya reached for her phone on the nightstand. "I turned it off before bed last night. I didn't want to talk to anyone."

She'd missed five calls: one from Travis and four from Jordan. The call from Travis came in the night before. That was good. It was before the photo went up. The ones from Jordan started ten minutes after the story posted and continued, like clockwork, every fifteen minutes. The last call had come in two minutes earlier.

"This is not good." Maya didn't bother listening to the messages. She hit return on Jordan's call. Travis was flying back this morning. She could wait to speak with him in person.

"It's going to be okay," Jordan said as she answered the phone. Maya was getting used to her lack of greetings. "Esteban is freaking out, but Esteban always freaks out."

Maya pulled the laptop back from Cleo. She couldn't imagine what the designer was upset about. Maya mostly covered Jake in the shot and all that could be seen of her dress was the left shoulder. The rest of the picture was "full of smoldering eyes and moistened lips"—to quote the caption under the picture.

Finally Maya had gotten that "smolder."

"What does this mean for the campaign?" Maya asked. She tried to keep it professional when all she truly wanted to know was what people were going to think of her.

"The fashion blogs are already lighting up about the dress," Jordan said.

Maya checked the article again. That was the only photo. "Did other pictures leak?"

"No. Just that one. But it's enough. So far everything has

been examined, from the material to the color. This story crosses from sports to fashion and everyone has an opinion."

"Are they going to scrap the campaign?" Maya wasn't sure what that meant for her payment if the photos never ran. There was something about that in the contract, she was sure, but she never completely understood the legal language it was written in. Another reason she had to make this agent decision sooner rather than later.

"They've invested too much already," Jordan assured her. "They'll probably just move it up and get the rest of the pictures out as soon as they can. Until then, they're working on damage control. I'll keep you posted."

Jordan was gone before Maya could thank her. She was torn between updating Cleo on the conversation and checking Travis's message. She didn't have a chance to do either when the phone rang again. The number on the screen was from the school switchboard, which meant it came from someone on campus. Normally, Maya didn't answer a call when she didn't know who was on the other end, but she had a sneaking suspicion this was one call she couldn't let roll over to voice mail.

"Maya, it's Nails Reed," Travis's dad said as she answered the phone.

"Hi, Mr. Reed."

"I'm assuming you've seen the article by now." Like Jordan, Nails didn't bother with pleasantries. "I'd like you to come to my office so we can discuss the situation."

"Okay," she said. "When would—"

"Now," he replied as he hung up.

Maya shook her head. "Nobody says good-bye anymore, do they?"

Maya was back in the principal's office. At least this time she knew for certain that she'd done nothing wrong. She didn't leak that picture to the Wall. She wasn't the "anonymous friend" who gave those quotes. She wasn't even dating Jake *or* Travis. And yet, she still felt everything was all her fault.

The door slammed open behind her, causing Maya to jump.

"I'm so sorry, Maya," Jake said as he came in. "I had nothing to do with that picture leaking."

The apology caught Maya off guard. "I never thought you did."

Jake sat in the chair beside her. "I wanted to make sure you knew I wasn't into playing games like some people. I'm just sorry this whole thing happened. I never should have taken this job."

Maya worried that the "some people" was a reference to Travis. Jake probably thought his brother was working with Nicole again, even though that made no sense at all. Travis had nothing to gain from this story.

"It's okay, Jake," Maya assured him. "No one could have anticipated this. And I needed the money. I'm glad you took the job."

He took her hands in his. "Well, I'm sorry anyway."

"You should be," Travis said from behind them.

"Travis?" Maya released Jake's hand.

"I go away for one day and you're moving in on Maya again," Travis said. "Unbelievable."

Jake stood to face his brother. "Moving in on her? I keep hearing that you two are just friends. How am I moving in on anything?"

"So you are going after her?"

"I told her I would."

It surprised Maya that he remembered that. He certainly hadn't been acting like it, no matter what he said while he fought with his brother. They continued yelling at each other, throwing accusations about Maya and things that had nothing to do with her. It wasn't odd to see Jake behave that way, but Travis was a shock. He was usually the calm, cool, and collected one in the family.

Nails seemed just as surprised as he watched his sons go at it from behind his desk, until finally he said, very softly, "Enough."

Travis and Jake stopped immediately.

Nails stood. "I'm glad you two got that out. Now it's over. Understood?" His voice never rose above a whisper.

"Yes, sir," both sons said in unison.

"I called you three here for damage control," Nails continued. "That is what we're going to do. First, this teenage melodrama is going to stop immediately. It was a photo shoot. I don't care what it looked like. Maya and Jake were performing for the camera. That's all it was. Don't turn it into a real story."

Maya squirmed in her seat. Nothing she'd felt had been a performance.

"No one will make any comments to the Wall or any other media outlet," Nails said. "The Academy Expo is coming up. If you have to ignore the reporters, that's what you're going to do. I don't want any of this coming back on our family or the school."

Maya knew she wasn't one of Nails's priorities, but it stung to hear him basically say that he wasn't worried about her at all.

"And I think Maya should stay away from the both of you for a while," Nails added. "At least until the story dies down."

"Dad!" Jake said.

"That's not fair," Travis added.

"I would think you had enough to worry about right now, Travis. If we learned anything from that disastrous spot on *The Hype*, it's that you need a little more time to concentrate on football and avoid pointless distractions."

Maya had obviously missed something. She felt particularly horrible about going to bed without catching up with Travis's appearance on the sports show.

Nails shuffled through the papers on his desk. He removed a pair of pages from the pile. "Travis . . . Maya . . . I've filled both your schedules with meetings and projects to prepare for the Expo next weekend. The two of you will be very busy. I'm sure Jake can find some distractions to occupy his time."

They all knew the word "distractions" was code for "girls." Jake's distractions were usually frowned upon, but Nails clearly wasn't above using that facet of his son's personality when it suited his needs.

Nails handed one of the pages to Maya, finally looking

directly at her. His expression softened, as did the tone of his voice. "I'm not blaming you for this, Maya. You're as much a victim here as anyone. More so, because you're the bigger name at the moment. I just feel it would be best to avoid giving this story legs. If there's really nothing to it, the media will move on quickly. Then you can all go on with your lives. Sound good?"

The three teens mumbled things that sounded like agreement and Nails dismissed them with a smile.

Jake tore out of the room without looking back. Maya felt like Travis was hanging around waiting for her as she put her schedule in her bag and got up from the chair. She didn't want Nails to see them walking out together since it was exactly the opposite of what he'd just told them to do, but there was no choice. Travis was holding the door waiting for her.

"I'm sorry about Dad," Travis said once the door was safely closed behind them.

"What is it with you guys apologizing for things you have no control over?" Maya said, attempting to add some levity to the mood.

"Guess Jake and I are more alike than any of us thought," Travis said. They fell into silence.

As they left the Administration building, Maya expected Travis to say good-bye and head in a different direction, but he stayed with her. The silence between them grew awkward.

"So, you saw *The Hype*?" Travis asked.

"I'm so sorry," she said. "Now it's my turn to apologize. Yesterday was so crazy with the shoot and . . . everything. I never had the chance to watch it."

"Then you were probably wondering what Dad was

talking about in there," Travis said as they made their way across campus.

She was afraid to ask. "It didn't go well?"

"It was horrible," Travis said. "The whole segment was about whether or not I was a real player or 'All Hype.'" He threw in air quotes to mock the show's signature segment in which a panel of judges discuss an up-and-coming star to decide if he or she is the real deal or not.

"They didn't tell you that you were part of that segment?"

Travis's body deflated. "No. When they first brought it up when I walked on set I thought I was one of the judges."

Maya was horrified for him. That was even more embarrassing than showing up on the Wall in some badly researched gossip story. This was about Travis as an athlete. That was far more important than who Maya was kissing.

"They just kept talking about my dad," Travis said. "Saying how no one would even know who I was if I didn't share his name."

"Obviously, they've never seen you play."

"That's the thing," he said. "They have! The judges all visited the school in the past year. One person on the panel did defend me. But even she brought up the times I've been on the Wall, saying how that was just 'Hyping me up.'" Again with the air quotes. Maya never realized how annoying the show's signature lines were until they were aimed at someone she cared about.

Maya had to ask the one question that she really, really didn't want to. "So . . . what did they decide? Are you 'All Hype' or not?"

“That’s the worst part,” he said, bringing his hands up again for another set of air quotes. “ ‘The jury’s still out.’ ”

Maya wrapped her arms around Travis. She didn’t care that they were in public, where any number of camera phones could snap shots of them. Her friend needed comfort.

“The jury’s still out” was the worst judgment anyone could get on the show. Saying someone was “Worth the Hype” was a badge of honor. “All Hype” could at least give a person something to be angry about, to show everyone how wrong they were. But “The jury’s still out” says they didn’t even care enough about Travis to decide.

“I should get to the gym,” Travis said as he pulled out of the hug. “I need to lift some weights.”

“Do that later,” Maya suggested. “Let’s get breakfast.”

“No. Dad’s right. I should focus more on my game.”

Even though Travis didn’t add in that he should spend less time with Maya, that unspoken part was all that she heard.

“Call me later,” she said. “Let me know how you’re doing.”

“Sure.” He threw on a smile. “And hey, that picture with you and Jake. Even though I hated to see it, you did look great. The ad campaign is going to be a success. And that’s all because of you.”

“Thanks,” Maya said. The campaign was the last thing she cared about.

Chapter 15

The scent of coffee woke Maya on Sunday. For a brief moment, she felt like she was home in Syracuse. She imagined being in her warm bed, with Dad making breakfast and Mom brewing up her signature French vanilla lattes on that crazy contraption she'd saved for months to buy. Seeing Cleo sitting on the edge of her bed with a to-go cup in her hand and a bright smile on her face was almost as nice.

Then Maya realized that Cleo's smile was just a little too bright. And that her computer was in her lap.

"What's on the Wall about me today?" Maya asked as she accepted the coffee. It tasted nothing like her mom's French vanilla latte.

"Nothing," Cleo quickly said. "Nothing at all."

"Then what's with the coffee run and why do you look like you're trying very hard not to kill someone?"

"I'd say the look is more one of regret that we haven't killed Nicole already."

Maya put the coffee down on her nightstand, suspecting she didn't want any hot liquid in her hands when she found out what was going on. "Tell me."

Cleo turned the laptop toward Maya. It was another article on the Wall, but Cleo was right. It wasn't about Maya at all.

An enormous picture of Nicole sat at the top of the page. She was out in front of some club smiling at the paparazzi like she was happy they were there. It made sense, since she obviously wanted to be seen, and Maya knew why.

Nicole was in Esteban's dress. The signature look from his collection. The one Maya was supposed to debut to the world in the ad campaign.

"That's my dress!" Maya said.

"I thought I recognized the shoulder," Cleo said. The joke fell over with a thud.

"That's *my* dress!" Maya insisted.

"Well, technically, it's Esteban's dress and he can do what he wants with it," Cleo reminded her.

Maya got off the bed. She needed to be on her feet. She needed to move. "That's not the point. I was supposed to launch the line in that dress. I was supposed to be the one in the picture."

"Okay, Maya, you need to breathe," Cleo said. "It's just a dress."

"No. It's Nicole taking something from me again." She grabbed her phone.

"Who are you calling?" Cleo asked.

"Nicole couldn't just reach into her closet and pull out that dress. Someone had to arrange for her to wear it." Maya hit Jordan's name on her favorites list. She'd just added the agent to that list and now she seriously considered wiping Jordan out of the phone completely.

"Maya, calm down before you talk to her," Cleo warned. "Jordan Cromwell is far more powerful than Nicole King."

Maya waited while the phone rang. "I'm not going to say anything stupid. But I do deserve an explanation."

Jordan's voice came on the line. "Good morning, Maya! How are you?"

"Um . . . fine. And you?" Maya was momentarily thrown. Jordan never answered the phone with a typical greeting, much less one that enthusiastic. She usually just started the conversation.

"Good," Jordan replied. "Enjoying a lazy Sunday, which is anything but lazy in this business we've decided to pursue."

Jordan was making small talk? Maya worried that she'd called the wrong Jordan.

"I'm glad you rang," Jordan said. "I was hoping to get in touch with you today."

"I saw the picture of Nicole in Esteban's dress."

"Yes," Jordan said. "Sorry about that. Esteban was beside himself over the leaked photo. And of course, the fashion community was ravenous to see more than that bit of sleeve. Getting that dress out in the public was the only way to deal with it. Creative Core could never pull together a suitable ad campaign fast enough to satiate that audience."

Maya nodded her head like she understood even though she knew Jordan couldn't see her. "But . . . is there some reason I couldn't wear it? I've been on the Wall, too."

"Yes, Maya. I'm sorry to say, but the reality is that you wearing the dress out on the town isn't a story," Jordan said.

"But Nicole wearing it is?"

"I knew you'd understand," Jordan said.

"I . . . But . . . Jordan—"

"Trust me, Maya. I've been doing this awhile now. We saved the campaign. That's the important part. Doesn't matter who's wearing the dress. You're going to be the face of Esteban's line. That's worth more than a picture on the Wall. Now, go enjoy your Sunday. Once this ad starts running, your schedule's going fill up."

Jordan reverted to form and hung up without saying good-bye or letting Maya get in a word. She still had plenty to say, but it was pointless. "*This is business, not high school*" echoed through her head. Jordan was right. She had to be a professional.

Maya picked up the computer to get a better look at the dress. She had to admit that Nicole looked good in it. But Maya looked better.

She was about to close the laptop when something other than the dress caught her attention. Nicole had a huge bracelet on the wrist that she'd been nursing for the past two weeks. It was just large enough to hide a small bandage. If Nicole had gone to see someone about the wrist, Maya would have heard. She knew firsthand how hard it was to keep anything a secret at that school. If the wrist still hurt Nicole two weeks after the match, the injury had to be serious.

Good, Maya thought. *She deserves it.* Then she immediately felt horrible for having that thought.

"Your agent was right," Renee said as they casually walked in the sunshine on streets miles away from the Academy and their classmates' cell phone cameras.

"She's not my agent yet," Maya quickly reminded her friend.

"Okay. Nicole's agent was right. It's a beautiful Sunday for relaxing."

"Ugh! Don't mention that name around me." Much as Maya didn't want to agree, the day was beautiful. Renee had offered to drive them out to the beach for brunch and Maya couldn't have been happier she'd agreed. The sun and the ocean were the perfect things to take her mind off the Wall.

It was still early for a lazy Sunday, so most people were home in bed. The sidewalk was light on foot traffic and the cars were few and far between. They had an unobstructed view of the ocean that stretched out till it met with the sky.

It was nice to get off campus and forget about classes and practices and the typical drama that seemed to be lurking around every corner. It was especially nice to not have to worry about Travis and Jake. They both had drills to run, so there would be no bumping into them at all, no matter how much a part of Maya secretly wished she could.

"How are things with Diego?" Cleo asked.

"Good?" Renee said.

"Is that an answer or a question?" Maya asked.

"Both?"

"What does that even mean?" Cleo asked.

"It means I'm confused," Renee admitted. "We haven't known each other all that long, but I think he wants a relationship."

"That's usually a good thing," Cleo said.

Renee glared at her. "I know! I'm just not used to it. Most guys get what they want, then move on. They don't usually stick around."

Maya hated hearing that. On the surface, Renee seemed to have more confidence than most of their classmates. But the people who knew Renee best understood that she was incredibly insecure. Maya appreciated that her friend was comfortable enough around them to let them see this personal side to her, but she wished it didn't exist.

"You better get used to it," Maya said. "I have a feeling Diego's not going anywhere."

Renee sat down on a bench so abruptly that Maya and Cleo had to stop and backtrack to keep with her. "That's what I'm afraid of," Renee said.

"You are officially making less sense than usual," Cleo said as she and Maya sat alongside their friend.

"I know!" Renee said. "He's totally messing with my mind."

"Don't blame this on Diego," Maya said. "You're doing this to yourself."

"I'm doing this to myself *because* of Diego," Renee said.

Cleo shook her head. "You're a mess."

"I won't argue with that," Renee said. "I like it better when I'm helping you with your problems. I don't want to be the one with the messed-up love life."

"Renee, the only thing messed up about your love life is

that you've got a guy who likes you—the real you," Maya said. "That's a good thing."

"I know! It's insane." Renee stood up just as abruptly as she'd sat down. "Come on. The restaurant's only a block away. I'm hungry."

Maya and Cleo shared a look of confusion. Neither of them was certain that they'd helped their friend through her mini freak-out, but Renee having an appetite was a good thing, so they went with it. The girls walked arm in arm, taking up most of the empty sidewalk as they continued to the restaurant.

"Maya! Maya!"

Maya broke away from her friends and turned toward the unfamiliar voice calling out her name. A man with a camera hurried toward her, clicking shots as he got closer.

"Do you know him?" Cleo asked.

"No," Maya said definitively. "But he sure knows me."

Renee clapped excitedly. "Your first paparazzi stalking! Congratulations."

"We should get inside," Cleo said.

"Agreed." Maya turned away from the man as the three of them quickened their pace.

"Maya, where's Travis this morning?" the man called after her. "How about Jake?"

"Don't say a thing," Cleo warned through clenched teeth.

"What did you think of Nicole King in that Esteban dress?" the man continued. "Who wore it better? You or her?"

Maya did her best to ignore him, but it was difficult. There was a line outside the restaurant. Maya wanted to push past everyone to get inside, but she could already see the article slamming her for being rude and jumping the line.

"Do you think the full pictures of you in that dress will ever see the light of day?"

That one hurt. Maya was worried about that. Jordan had said the ad campaign was going forward. But now that the Wall had provided free advertising—not to mention the sites that picked up the picture afterward—why would the ad agency pay to have Maya's photo splashed all over the place?

Renee leaned in to whisper to Maya. "He's trying to get a rise out of you; make you do something picture-worthy. Keep ignoring him."

Everyone on the restaurant patio was staring. The line to get in wasn't moving any faster.

"Come on, give me something," the man pleaded. "What do you think of your anonymous friend Nicole?"

The words slipped out before Maya could stop them. "Anonymous friend?"

The man smiled like a cat that had caught its canary. "From the story about you and the Reed brothers. You knew Nicole King was the anonymous friend, right?"

Maya had suspected as much. It wasn't really a surprise. But it was still tough to hear from a total stranger. Maya knew he was baiting her. She understood that was part of the game. But, suddenly, she simply didn't care anymore.

"I'm more worried about Nicole's injury than I am some dress," Maya said. "If she doesn't get that wrist taken care of, I'm afraid of what could happen to her career."

Too late, Maya realized the clicks had stopped even though the camera was still aimed at her. Her eyes went wide as she realized it was a video camera as well. She'd been hoping to give him a bit of hearsay to report back to the Wall. She hadn't intended to give him an actual sound bite to post instead.

"Ms. Hart," another stranger's voice called out to her. The hostess pushed her way past the line of people still waiting to get in. "Your table's ready. Right this way."

Maya was pretty sure they hadn't made a reservation. The kind woman had seen her in need, recognized her, and come to render aid. Maya felt incredibly lucky.

As she watched the paparazzo hurry off with his camera, she also felt incredibly guilty.

Chapter 16

"Whether it was your plan or not, you definitely got people to stop talking about you and the Reed boys," Renee said as she and Maya entered Watson Hall. Renee had been hanging out there for the past couple days to avoid Nicole. She and Cleo were both clearly in the video with Maya when she outed Nicole's injury. All three girls had been lying low ever since, hoping to avoid Nicole's wrath.

"There was no plan, Renee. You were there. You saw what happened!" Maya still felt terrible. The story about Nicole's wrist was on the Wall before they'd even finished brunch. That lovely little video of Maya—with more anger than concern in her voice—had been the talk of the Academy by the time they rolled back through the gates of the school.

It was now spinning out of control. Gossipmongers came out of the woodwork theorizing about what was wrong with

Nicole, why she kept it a secret, and if it was a career-ending situation as Maya had suggested.

"What I don't get," Maya said, "is why she refuses to deal with the problem. It might just be some minor thing."

"Because Nicole King never shows weakness," Renee explained. "With her it's always attack, never surrender. You should know better than anyone. Nicole doesn't set out to deal with a problem. She does everything she can to make sure the problem never exists in the first place."

"What a horrible way to live," Maya said.

"That's part of sports," Renee said. "It's part of competition."

"I don't know that I'm cut out for that side of the business," Maya said.

Jordan had been livid. Not only had Maya sunk to Nicole's level, but she'd completely failed to give Jordan the heads-up on her other client. To be fair, Maya had a problem getting a word in edgewise when she spoke with Jordan, which she would have pointed out if the agent hadn't abruptly hung up the phone again.

"Maybe now at least Jordan can force Nicole to have the injury checked," Maya said, trying to put a positive spin on the situation as they reached her room.

"Yeah, I'm just going to hang here until things calm down back the villa," Renee said.

Maya pushed the door open. She was about to suggest that Renee might be hiding from Diego as well, when she realized Cleo was in the middle of a video chat with her parents back in China. Usually, Maya had some warning in advance when a call like that happened. Getting a connection through to Cleo's family was a lot more difficult than Maya getting in touch with her folks in Syracuse.

The girls entered the room quietly, careful not to interrupt. Maya didn't speak a word of Chinese, but she could tell something was wrong by the stern tones that Cleo's parents had adopted and the pleading way their daughter responded. This was not the typical, strong-willed Cleo that Maya recognized. This was a little girl being scolded.

Cleo's parents raised their voices. It wasn't anger that Maya heard. It was concern. That parental tone was universal no matter the language. Renee recognized it as well, turning to Maya and raising her eyebrows quizzically. Maya worried that she knew what the talk was about, but didn't say anything. She went over to her bed and sat quietly while she waited for the call to end. Renee joined her.

The conversation didn't go on much longer once they were in the room. The tone became softer, less stressed, as Cleo and her parents said their good-byes. Cleo closed the connection, then paused for a beat, refusing to turn around and acknowledge that her friends were in the room. Maya and Renee waited silently until she was ready to talk.

Cleo took a deep, cleansing breath and turned to face her friends. Her eyes were full of rage. "I'm going to kill him."

"Kill who?" Renee asked.

Maya was pretty sure she knew. "Grant Adams?"

"Somehow," Cleo said. "*Somehow* my parents, who live in China . . . who don't have a computer of their own, much less an Internet connection . . . *somehow* they've gotten wind of his post that questions my commitment to my Chinese heritage. The one that asks if I'm 'too Americanized.' "

"Oh, no," Renee said.

"They practically ran to the nearest Internet café to talk to me," Cleo said.

"That's explains the sudden call," Maya said. "How bad is it?"

"They're not mad," Cleo said. "They're disappointed. They're worried. This is why they were afraid to send me so far from home."

"They were afraid you'd become American?" Maya asked.

Cleo rolled her eyes. It was actually nice to see the assertive Cleo back. "They're afraid I'd become everything. A partier. Hooked on drugs. Start liking girls."

"But you're not those things," Maya said. "Well, except the last one. You don't do any of that."

"That's not what Grant Adams thinks."

"Who cares what some person you've never met thinks?"

"It's not just Adams." Cleo pulled up the blog to the most recent entry, a collection of her looks from the last week, including a grab from the video of her at brunch. The winner of the interview with Adams had snagged a picture of her in her prison-suit pajamas brushing her teeth in the dorm bathroom. "Look at these comments. Ninety-five percent of them are trashing me for being who I am. Maybe they're right."

Maya didn't need to look at the screen. "Don't be ridiculous. You can't hide who you are."

"Not hide it," Cleo said. "Just dress it up differently. Look more like the rest of the women on the pro tour. I can still be myself when the cameras aren't around."

"When aren't the cameras around?" Renee asked pointedly. Maya couldn't help but notice that she'd been unusually quiet through most of the conversation. But Renee was right. Grant Adams had seen to it that cameras followed Cleo all over campus.

"Good point," Cleo said. "I might have to tone down my look altogether, but especially when I'm on the course."

"Cleo, you have to be true to yourself," Maya insisted. "You can't let Grant Adams and people like him win."

"Honestly, Maya, I only care about winning and losing on the golf course. I didn't abandon my family and move to the other side of the world to get my picture on the Wall. I did it to play golf. To be the best."

"Being the best has nothing to do with the way you look," Maya said.

"I think Renee would disagree with you," Cleo said.

Both of them turned to Renee, who had suddenly become very interested in her shoes.

"Renee?" Maya prodded.

She raised her head. "Cleo's right. No one's talking about her game. They're just trashing her look."

Maya groaned. "Unbelievable!"

"I'm not saying you're wrong, Maya," Renee said. "But there are certain realities that Cleo needs to deal with. The pro-golf circuit is not ready for their own Lady Gaga."

"Hey! I'm not that crazy with costumes."

"Cleo, one side of your head has dark black spiky hair while the other half is long, flowing blue-and-red locks with the roots starting to show."

"I'm letting it grow out," Cleo said.

"If you worked in the music industry, no one would bat an eye," Renee said. "You're not trying to get into the music industry."

"So, what?" Maya asked. "She needs a makeover?"

"More like a make*under*," Renee said. "And she needs to do it before the Expo this weekend. There's going to be a ton of press on campus. It's the perfect place to debut her new look."

Silence fell on the room once again. Cleo had to make this decision on her own. She didn't need her friends adding extra pressure.

She looked in the mirror, running her hand through the long hair on the side of her head. "Fine, Renee. Do what you want."

Maya checked the clock. Cleo and Renee had been gone for over an hour. She'd asked to come along, too, but Renee had forbidden it. She'd told Maya that it was going to be hard enough work convincing Cleo to make the changes to her style. She didn't need to deal with Maya's disapproval the whole time.

Maya did disapprove, but she was also resigned to the fact that it was what Cleo wanted. It might be a mistake, but it was Cleo's mistake to make. Besides, Maya had interfered in enough lives this week.

The familiar chime of an e-mail coming in drew Maya's

attention to her computer. Her e-mail popularity had quadrupled since she was named Student Ambassador for the Academy Expo. She and Travis were cc'd on every major and minor decision the staff made, even though they were rarely invited to share their opinion.

Maya had been relegated to minor tasks like choosing the gift bags for the celebrity participants. She didn't have anything to do with the gifts. She only got to pick out the bags.

Every time she mentioned it, the adults assured her that she'd have a major role on the day of the Expo. She and Travis would be the public faces of the event. It would have meant more if she'd been allowed to see Travis before the event happened.

It was like Nails had sent out a memo to the staff to keep Maya away from his sons. They didn't have any classes together and their practice schedules kept them apart on the six-hundred-acre Academy. It was still odd that she hadn't even bumped into either brother for the past couple days.

The e-mail was another one for Maya to store in her Expo folder. It was getting to the point that she barely read them, but this one caught her attention. It was the schedule of events for the day. Finally, Maya would know what celebrity she'd be playing against!

She opened the document and scanned through the list. Every sport would be featured, so the day was packed with events. Maya started to worry when she didn't come across her name, but the fear was pointless. Not only was Maya on the list, she was part of the finale!

"Primrose!" she shouted to no one. "Oh my God!

Primrose!" Maya was bouncing in her chair with excitement. She wanted to shout some more, but held back. It wasn't very ambassadorial behavior, especially if the other girls on her floor heard her. But it was incredibly exciting news.

The biggest stars on the *planet* were going to be at the Expo—and Maya was going to play with them! Primrose, the multiplatinum teen pop duo, were booked to close out the day in a doubles tennis match that *everyone* would want to see. And not just because the reigning pop princesses currently had the number-one album on the charts.

Nails Reed knew exactly what he was doing when he put together the schedule. It wasn't enough that the most popular stars at the Expo would be the finale. That wouldn't truly showcase his school. He had to add a little something extra for that. Something the sports community and anyone who read the Wall would want to see. Maya was paired up with Vanessa Primrose, while her sister, Miranda, was partnered with Nicole.

The excitement Maya felt for getting to meet Vanessa and Miranda was tempered by the knowledge that she was going to have to go up against Nicole after outing her injury. This was not good.

Nicole would be gunning for Maya, throwing everything she had into the match to demolish her enemy and put an end to the questions about her wrist once and for all. If Maya beat her, she'd forever be the girl who played against an injured Nicole and possibly damaged the star's career. There was no way she could win this match, no matter what the final scoreboard said.

Maya tried to push those concerns from her mind as she

scanned the rest of the list to see what the day held in store. Her co-ambassador, Travis, was scheduled for a flag football game against a team composed of the hottest actors on the CW. Maya was surprised to see Jake's name there, too, as she was almost certain that Nails still considered his more emotional son a risk when it came to putting him in front of the cameras on the field. Then again, promoting the Reed name trumped all other concerns.

Except for the stand-alone tennis finale, the rest of the events overlapped as the day played out. Cleo's golf outing alone took up most of the day, giving fans the chance to stop in for a bit between other games. This probably maximized the school's ability to showcase as many students as possible. It was a good setup, but Maya quickly realized something was missing from the schedule.

Maya read through the document again to make sure she hadn't overlooked anything.

"Oh, no," she said, but not nearly as loudly as her last outburst. *This is not good.*

Renee's name was not on the schedule for the swim meet. She wasn't included in the day at all.

How in the world would Maya tell her?

The door banged open and Cleo jumped into the room. "Ta-da!"

"Oh my God!" Maya's hand flew to her mouth in shock.

The long, red-and-blue side of Cleo's hair was completely gone. It had been chopped off and buzz cut down so that her whole head was covered by half-inch spiky black hair. "That's amazing!"

"It was all we could do, really," Renee said with a sigh. "She's put so many chemicals in that hair already I was afraid of what another color treatment would do."

"It looks cool," Maya said. "But I don't think Grant Adams will approve."

Renee pulled a pink baseball cap out of her bag and placed it on Cleo's head. "That's why we have this."

The cap did the trick. It drew all the attention away from Cleo's spiky hair, providing a properly subdued look. The pink cap looked odd topping off Cleo's outfit. She wore the same vintage jeans and tank top she'd left in.

Renee caught Maya looking at the clothes. "Yeah. The clothes are going to take a bit more work. I didn't have anything in my closet boring enough for the golf course."

"So we came back here to rifle through yours!" Cleo added.

Maya sneered at her friends with mock offense. But they were right. Out of the three of them, Maya was the only one whose everyday style would pass for . . . traditional.

Maya held a hand out toward her closet. "Have at it."

"Thanks, Maya!" Cleo said as she dove for the clothes.

As Renee went to join her, Maya grabbed her friend by the arm, stopping her. "Renee, I've got something to tell you."

Renee called out to Cleo. "Don't you hate it when people announce they have to tell you something? Nothing good ever comes after that."

Maya sighed. She wasn't supposed to reveal the schedule to any of her classmates. That was for the coaches to do. But Maya couldn't keep that kind of information from one of her best friends. "I got the schedule for Saturday."

"Let me guess . . . I'm not on it?"

"Renee, I'm so sorry, but—"

Renee held up a hand to stop her. "It's okay. I suspected as much. The Academy wants to show off the best and the brightest. We all know that's not me."

"Bull!" Cleo said from the closet. Half the contents of Maya's hangers were already on her bed. "We just have to—"

"No," Renee said. "We don't have to do anything. I don't want to embarrass myself in front of some celebrity or the press. My parents would probably prefer me to disappear into the background rather than having some blogger attack me the way they've been going after Cleo. This is probably for the best, really."

Maya didn't know what to say. "Renee, I could talk to—"

"Maya, I really am okay with this," Renee said. "Besides, now I won't have to miss Diego's game. In fact, I think I just came up with the perfect way to show him how much I'm invested in this relationship. This is going to work out great!"

Chapter 17

Maya sat on the makeshift stage half listening to Nails Reed's welcome speech. It was hard to concentrate on anything other than the ridiculousness of his latest plot to keep her and Travis apart. Nails had them sitting as far from each other as they possibly could, on the exact opposite sides of the stage. One thing was certain: no photos of Maya and Travis together would come out of this opening ceremony.

"So, please have fun today," Nails said, wrapping up his speech. "Explore the campus. Meet our students and staff. And watch some celebrities get a taste of what it's like to take on future sports stars."

The crowd applauded politely before they dispersed to various points of the campus. A special app had been created for the Expo with a map of the campus and the times of the events along with directions to get from one venue to another. Maya was going to be busy making appearances at each of the overlapping events, which was likely part of Nails's plan as well.

Maya didn't care about that plan anymore. She hadn't talked to Travis all week and wanted to know how he was doing. There weren't any other pictures of them on the Wall, but the fallout from his appearance on *The Hype* hadn't died down. Travis was finally getting the amount of press coverage that his father wanted. It just wasn't the kind of stories he'd imagined.

It didn't matter that the press was out in force. A few shots of Maya and Travis talking together at school wasn't exactly breaking news. She had to find out how he was doing no matter what Nails thought about it. She was about to march right over to Travis, when she heard his father's voice behind her. "Maya?"

She considered ignoring him and walking away, but that would have been pushing it too far. Maya plastered a fake smile on her face and turned. "Yes?"

Her eyes went wide as she saw that Nails was not alone. Her new friend from the Ontario Open had made good on her promise to stop by the school. "Dona! I didn't know you were going to be here."

"It was a sudden decision." The tennis phenom placed a hand on Nails's arm. "*Someone* guilted me into it by reminding me how the additional press will bring more donations to help the students of this *fine institution*."

"Well, you can't say I wasn't right." Nails nodded to the many cameras and camera phones recording their reunion. "I'll leave you two to catch up."

"How do you put up with all this?" Maya said about the cameras.

"You learn to tune them out," Dona replied. "Most of the time."

Dona guided Maya to an area behind the stage that was mostly hidden from prying eyes. "On a related note, I was wondering how you were doing after that thing with Nicole online."

"You saw that?" Maya asked. Of course she had. *Everyone* had.

"I'm guessing it wasn't your proudest moment."

Maya shook her head. "She just gets to me."

"You're not the only one," Dona said, lowering her voice. Even though they were away from the crowds, she was still being careful. "Nicole doesn't have the best reputation on the tour. She's not like you."

"Not like me?" Maya asked, matching Dona's softer tone. There was something that had been in the back of Maya's mind since their press conference in Toronto. Only now did Maya realize it. She needed an answer to a question she didn't even know she'd had. "Don't get me wrong. I appreciate the compliment, but how do you know? We barely spoke in Toronto. And then you went and gave me your endorsement—"

"We talked on the court," Dona said. "Through our game. The way we played. That was all I needed to get a read on you, Maya. I've been doing this awhile. I even went up against Ms. King in her first professional tournament. Trust me, I can spot the difference. You have the hunger, but I don't expect it to devour you. It's something that I hope I've managed to keep myself after all my many years on the courts."

"It hasn't been *that many* years," Maya said.

"True. I might even have a few more good ones left, no matter what the press might say." She raised her voice back to a more conversational level. "But look, I don't want to keep you. You've got a lot to do today before you wipe the floor with Nicole this afternoon!"

"Dona!"

"Oh, whatever." She waved off the concern. "The cameras aren't within earshot. And even if they were, I don't care. Nicole's been playing up that wrist all week, like it's some kind of excuse for not beating me faster."

"I'm no fan of Nicole's," Maya said. "Not anymore. But she hasn't been playing it up. If anything, she's been hiding it from everyone. She still won't talk about it."

"Exactly," Dona said. "Which is why everyone is still talking about it. Trust me, Maya. This story isn't over."

Dona's warning followed Maya across campus as she made her way to the soccer field. Nails had scheduled a brief board meeting once the morning photo ops were done, but Dona planned to visit with Maya later in the day. She promised to give Maya all the advice she could about the wild and wacky world of the pro-tennis circuit. Until then, Maya tried to put all distractions out of her mind and enjoy the day.

The soccer game was already in full swing by the time Maya reached the field. The stands were filled with telenovela fans, since the Academy soccer team was taking on the cast of one of the most popular Spanish soap operas. Some of those fans even knew Diego already. They held handmade signs professing their love to the actors and that one particular soccer player.

Renee stood at the top of the stands, ignoring all the signs. It was one thing for those random girls—and a few guys—to dream of Diego, but she actually *had* him.

"What's that?" Maya asked when she saw the metal contraption Renee had set up. It held a computer tablet high enough to clear the signs, giving it a direct line of sight to the field.

Renee walked Maya a few steps away from the tablet. "Cleo's across-the-globe call the other day inspired me. I set up my own international video chat."

"You've decided this is the best way to introduce your family to Diego?"

"Oh, God no! But I did introduce myself to his," Renee said. "I snuck into his phone and got his cousin's e-mail address. We messaged back and forth to set up a surprise for Diego and his family. I rented out a local restaurant in a nicer part of town down there. It's a sports bar where they show soccer games from all over the world. I'm sending a live feed of the game so his family can watch him. They've never missed a single one of his games back home."

"Wow. You really do like this guy."

Renee looked back to the tablet, then leaned in to whisper to Maya. "I think I might do more than *like* him."

"You mean you might *love* him?"

Renee slapped a hand over Maya's mouth. "Don't say it out loud!"

Maya laughed while she batted Renee's hand away. "Doesn't matter if I say it or not. You're the one who has to say it for it to mean anything."

"It's way too soon."

"True," Maya agreed. "But the heart does not keep to a clock."

"It doesn't like being split in two either," Renee said. "What's the latest on the Reed boys?"

Maya turned her attention to the field. "Oh, look, your boyfriend has the ball and is taking it toward the net."

"You can put off the conversation with me, Maya," Renee said. "But you can't put it off with Travis much longer."

Maya made her way to the golf course a few minutes before the soccer game ended. The results of the game were already a foregone conclusion. Diego and the rest of the Academy team were letting the actors win.

It hadn't been obvious to most of the people in the stands at first, but anyone who'd ever seen a game played by Academy students knew it without question. They made far too many mistakes and missed too many opportunities. As the game went on, the mistakes became bigger and harder to miss. The Academy team switched from playing to performing.

It began with Diego doing a pratfall as he ran to the net. He tripped, fell, and tumbled past the goalie as the ball bounced off the post and back into the field of play. That inspired the rest of the team to one-up one another with more spectacular mistakes until even the actors laughed along. By the time Maya left the stands, the guests had outscored the Academy team by ten points.

The golf course was much calmer. However, a foursome that included a pair of designers from some fashion reality contest were adding a level of drama to the game, if the texts Maya was receiving were to be believed.

Maya hoped for a report when she caught up with Cleo at the ninth hole. A light lunch had been set out under tents there, since it was the midpoint of the game. Assorted members of the press were permitted to stage impromptu interviews there as well. Nails was not about to let any opportunity to promote his students—and his school—pass by.

Cleo had just finished at the ninth hole with an impressive eagle, putting the ball into the hole at two strokes under par. She received a polite round of applause from the crowd and smiled as she shook hands with her teammates, another girl from their class and two women who hosted a popular antiques show on PBS.

The fake smile dropped to an expression of extreme loathing as Cleo walked off the green and joined her friend. Dressed in Maya's pink polo and khaki shorts with Renee's baseball cap on top covering her buzz cut, Cleo was almost unrecognizable.

"Kill me," Cleo said by way of greeting. "Kill me now. Anything to end this torture."

Maya tried not to be too offended. "My clothes aren't *that* bad."

"It's not the clothes," Cleo said. "It's the company. Those

are two of the most boring people on the planet. They don't talk about anything but hundred-year-old chairs, and tapestries, and armoires—my God, the armoires! It never stops. How these people don't put their audiences to sleep every night is beyond me."

"At least you won't be showing up on the Wall with them," Maya said over a loud outburst of cheers and laughter from the crowd watching the ninth hole.

The designers Maya had been getting reports about were on the green behind Cleo's foursome. Well, one of them was on the green. The other one, dressed in plaid capris and a matching jaunty golf hat, was up in a tree trying to knock loose her golf ball, totally playing it up for the crowd.

"*Those* are the people I wish I'd been teamed with," Cleo said.

Maya cringed inwardly from guilt. She and her friends had promised to never keep secrets, but she was not planning to tell her roommate that those were the people Cleo *had* been teamed with. As Student Ambassador, Maya didn't have the power to get Renee on the swim roster, but she could rearrange the celebrity pairings on the golf course. She did just that the morning after Cleo's makeunder.

Maya still didn't agree with Cleo's plan to change up her look, but she wanted to be supportive. Those designers had developed a reputation on their show for flamboyance. They did whatever it took for extra screen time, from crazy outfits to backstabbing behavior. It was too big a risk to pair them with Cleo. The antiques show hosts were safer. No way they'd give Grant Adams anything to write about.

Seeing the designers on the course, Maya was glad she made the roster change to protect Cleo's reputation. But she was extremely sorry for the incredible drop in the fun factor of Cleo's afternoon. The designers were having a blast.

"Quick," Cleo said as she grabbed a glass of purple punch. "Tell me I look great."

Without hesitation, Maya said, "You look dreadful."

"Hey! I'm in your clothes."

"Yes. *My* clothes. You should be in your own. This is a stupid plan. I'm sorry I had anything to do with it."

"I have gotten more compliments on my game today than I've ever gotten before," Cleo said. "Obviously I'm doing something right."

"But at what cost?" Maya asked.

An older woman in khaki pants and a beige jacket over a green polo was very obviously eavesdropping on their conversation. "Can I help you?" Cleo asked.

"I'm sorry," the woman said. "I couldn't help but overhear. If you don't mind me saying so, I think it's a vast improvement over your old look. I saw you in that garish monstrosity in Savannah."

"Garish monstrosity?" Cleo said. "You must read Grant Adams. He called it that too."

"I've been known to peruse the blog," the woman admitted.

"Well," Maya said, "if *you* don't mind, I have to ask . . . don't you think he's been a little rough on a teenage girl?"

"I'm sure he's just trying to make a point," the woman said. "His advice is in her best interest. Your friend is quite proficient in the gentleman's game."

"Don't you think maybe it's time to stop calling it a gentleman's game?" Maya asked.

"It's just a figure of speech," the woman replied. "Not everything needs to be politically correct twaddle nowadays."

"You sound a lot like Grant Adams." Cleo's eyes narrowed. "Like maybe you *are* Grant Adams."

Maya had to laugh. "Cleo, don't be—" The deer-in-the-headlights look that flashed across the woman's face stopped Maya in her tracks. Was this woman really the man who had been attacking Cleo for the past two weeks?

"I don't know what you're talking about," the woman said.

"I've been doing a lot of research on 'Mr.' Adams lately," Cleo said. "The way you talk. The language you use. It's just like him. So, either you're a really devout follower, or . . ."

The woman didn't say anything, but she looked extremely uncomfortable.

Maya was outraged. "Why would you do that?" she asked the woman. "Why would you say those things? Why do you pretend to be a guy while you do it?"

The woman pointed at Cleo. "To protect her," she finally said. "I understand your position, Cleo. You're young. You have an amazing talent. And you think that will be enough to succeed. Not in this world, my dear.

"I call it the gentleman's game, because it still is a gentleman's game," the woman said. "There are rules that we must abide by if we want to excel. You will not get very far in this sport with preposterous hair and outlandish clothing."

"And if it means changing who I am, I should do that," Cleo said.

"It has worked for me," the woman agreed.

"Thank you," Cleo said with a smile. "I appreciate the advice."

Cleo put down her drink and walked back to the ninth hole. The designer who hadn't climbed into the tree was down on the ground, using her golf club like a pool cue to knock the ball into the hole.

Maya followed. "Cleo, where are you going?"

"I have a few minutes between holes," Cleo said. "I think it's time for another change."

Chapter 18

Maya was late for the beach volleyball match, but it didn't matter. She had to see what those fashion contest designers did with Cleo. They'd taken her back behind the trees so she could have her big reveal when they were done, but it was taking forever. Both their foursomes were supposed to be onto the second half of the course. Maya was concerned that Nails would blame her for the delay in the schedule.

Any thought for herself went out of Maya's head when she saw Cleo come out of the trees. Her friend looked comfortable for the first time since she put on Maya's outfit that morning. The old Cleo was back and better than ever. Maya's borrowed clothing, however, was completely unrecognizable.

Maya's shorts were artistically cut to give the bland khakis a bit of an edge with tiger stripes down the sides, showing just the right amount of skin. The sleeves on the polo were completely gone, emphasizing the biceps that Cleo had developed from swinging clubs for a large chunk of her life. The pink shirt faded into a purple-stained design, courtesy of that awful punch. Maya didn't want to think what that stuff did inside a person's body. Renee's baseball cap was gone completely, leaving Cleo's short spiky hair free for all to gawk at.

It was over the top, while still having nods to a classic look. Cleo had rarely looked better and Maya wondered why the designers hadn't won their season of the show.

Maya could barely contain herself as Cleo approached. "You look—"

"I know!"

"Wow."

They laughed at their sudden inability to create complex sentences. Cleo worked that outfit unlike anything their more fashionable friend, Renee, had ever worn.

Once the excitement passed, Maya took it down to a serious tone. "Are you ready for this?"

"Let Grant Adams come after me," Cleo said. "I'm not letting her make her issues mine."

Maya wanted see the rest of the game, but she'd already stayed beyond her scheduled allotment of time. There was still an afternoon full of appearances to make before meeting up with Nicole and Primrose.

Nails had done an impressive job creating a schedule that kept her and Travis on complete opposite sides of campus all day. There was no way the manipulative former football star could keep her from his son's game, though.

Maya breezed by the beach volleyball game, the swim meet, and a half-dozen track-and-field events before arriving at the football field at the start of halftime. She found Renee and Diego in the stands, holding hands and looking annoyingly adorable together. She was glad to see that things were working out between them, and happier that they remembered to save her a seat by the fifty yard line so she didn't have to fight for some square inch of the bleachers. The stands were packed.

With most of the other events wrapped up, the football field was the natural place for everyone to gather. It also boasted the second-largest celebrity draw of the day with the CW hotties.

Along the sidelines on the other side of the field, the most popular actresses from the network cheered on their costars. Cheerleading was one of the few sports that hadn't come to the Academy yet, so the "home" side of the field sat empty. Unfortunately for Maya, that meant there was nothing to drown out the conversations taking place around her.

"Oh, yeah! It was totally my idea for Travis to go on *The Hype*," Nicole said from her seat directly behind Renee, Diego, and Maya. "I suggested it to Tommy Z. He's one of the producers."

It reminded Maya of the conversation she'd overheard back at the tournament when those strangers had been complimenting Maya by way of trashing Nicole. The main difference was that Maya was fairly certain she was meant to overhear this talk.

"Nicole, that's horrible! You suggested Travis for *The Hype* judging?"

Maya didn't recognize the second voice, but it didn't matter.

It was just some random person Nicole had picked so she wasn't mumbling this information out loud by herself.

"Of course not!" Nicole said as if she were insulted by the suggestion. It wasn't the first time Maya had been impressed by her acting skills. "If I ever suspected that was going to happen, I would have told Travis to blow it off entirely. I should really call Tommy and give him hell for what he did to my friend."

"You're such a thoughtful person, Nicole."

Blech. Maya wondered if she'd sounded like that when she was under Nicole's spell. She didn't want to admit it to herself, but she probably had.

"I better get going," Nicole said. "I've got some things to arrange before the tennis match."

Maya refused to glance Nicole's way as she heard the metallic footsteps move past her and down the bleachers.

"And . . . scene!" Renee said once Nicole was safely out of earshot.

"Oh good," Maya said. "I wasn't the only one to suspect that performance was for our benefit."

Renee shook her head. "Nicole's been dropping hints about it all week. Just another reason I tried to avoid her."

"What's the point?" Maya asked. "None of it even matters."

"The only important thing is that that show affected Travis's game," Diego said. "Unless all this talk I heard about him being a star player really was because of his dad."

"No. He's good," Renee said. "He's just not good today."

Maya was afraid to ask. "How bad is it?"

Renee and Diego shared a look. They both obviously

wanted the other one to answer the question. Finally, Diego gave in. "At first, I thought he was messing around like we did in the soccer game—throwing way off target, stumbling backward and tripping over his own feet. But I don't think any of that was on purpose."

"They've been chanting 'Hype' all through the first half," Renee added. "The crappy D-list comedian the school got to be the game announcer started it up. Travis's game got worse the more they yelled . . . and the worse his game got, the more they shouted it."

Maya glanced to the scoreboard. There were still a few minutes left of halftime. Since this wasn't a serious game, the guys stayed on the field during the break. The CW actors were on their side of the field posing for pictures with the fans.

"I should talk to him," Maya said.

"That's the last thing you should do," Diego said.

"Nails will kill you," Renee added.

"I've done what Nails wanted all week long," Maya reminded them. "I stayed away. It didn't make any difference."

Maya got up before Renee could talk her out of it. She used to have a calming presence on Jake. Maybe that would work with Travis as well. Even if it didn't, she couldn't just sit there and watch Travis fall apart through the second half without trying something.

Maya was thankful that the CW girls were putting on some kind of halftime show. Most of the people in the stands were watching their performance instead of Maya walking to the sideline. She got there in time to catch the tail end of the coach's inspirational speech to his players. Nails had decided to lead the Academy guys for this exhibition match.

"I know this isn't a real game," Nails said. "But are we going to let those pretty-boy actors make us look like amateurs?"

"No!" the guys yelled in response.

"Darn right we aren't," Nails said. "We are warriors. That is *our* battlefield. Are we going to let them take it from us?"

"No!" the team shouted again.

"Back when I was playing, we had a little ritual in the locker room during halftime," Nails said. "That's when the coach would name his own MVP for the game. Someone to lead the team out for the second half. Well, I'm going to do that now."

Maya hung back and listened, imagining all the ways what Nails was about to say could go wrong.

"I know this is going to seem biased," Nails said. "But I don't care. We all know who the leader on that field has been in the first half and I'm not afraid to say it just because he's my son." Nails's hand came down on Jake's shoulder. "Jake, continue to do me proud."

The only person who looked more surprised than Jake was Travis. They were both speechless as Nails led the team in a final chant before breaking the group to get ready for the second half.

Nails saw Maya before his sons did. He glared at her, but didn't say anything in front of the guys. That was good, because she was even more concerned about Travis when she saw him standing alone staring out at the field.

"Hey," Maya said as she reached him.

Travis grunted in return.

They stood together in silence. After a week of avoiding each other, Maya found they had nothing to say. It didn't help that the halftime show had ended and it felt like everyone in the stands was watching them. At first, Maya thought it was just her imagination, but the number of cell phone cameras trained on them proved she had a right to be paranoid.

Maya didn't want to start with the obvious, but the staring into space was already beyond awkward. "How's the game going?"

"I'd rather not talk about it."

"It's a good turnout," Maya said. "I'd call this day a success."

"Maya, I need to concentrate. Can we save this for after the game?"

"Oh," Maya said. "Sure."

She should have listened to Renee. The walk back to the stands was going to be even more awkward than the standing in silence. Thankfully, Jake nodded her over before she would have to make that walk. That was both a good thing and a bad one.

"I've never seen him like this," Jake said softly, knowing that they were in a very public space.

"Reminds me of someone else I know," Maya said.

"Maybe we're more alike than I thought," Jake said. "That would explain some things."

Maya couldn't help but think that she was one of those things.

"You know," Jake said, "that's the first time my dad has praised my playing in a long time. Figures he'd use it as a back-handed compliment to smack Travis around."

"It doesn't matter why he said it, Jake. He said it. Eventually you'll find a way to make him believe it."

Jake smiled. "I don't know what it is about this messed-up family that keeps you interested."

Maya smiled along with him. "Believe me, Jake, I wish I knew."

If the third quarter was any indication of how the first half had gone, Maya was glad she'd missed it. Travis was so far out of the zone, Maya thought someone else was playing entirely.

It didn't help that the announcer was squarely on the side of the actors. He'd been razzing the Academy players every chance he got.

Travis threw another long, wobbly pass. It wasn't pretty and it wasn't anywhere near a player. But unofficial MVP Jake saw the opportunity and made an incredible running leap. He snagged the ball out of the air and held tight as he came down, rolling to the ground before popping back up on his feet. An actor's hand just brushed his side, pulling the flag from his belt, stopping the play dead.

If it had been tackle football, Jake would have been able to run it into the end zone. An incredible catch made even more spectacular by a touchdown. As it was, it still gave the announcer a way to turn something good into something bad.

"Looks like one Reed brother really is worth the hype!"

High fives switched to balled-up fists as the celebration turned dark. Maya obviously couldn't hear what was being said, but it was clear that there was trash talk happening. One of the actors, who probably thought he was just having fun being one of the guys, made a comment. Travis said something back with a flash of anger across his face that brought Jake hurrying over to talk him down.

The ball was on the five yard line. Any other time, it would have been an easy play. The Academy students could practically walk it in against a team of actors. But nothing looked easy at the moment.

Travis almost vibrated on the turf. He jumped from foot to foot, unable to stand still. Maya had watched enough football games in her time at the Academy to know that this was not ideal for the quarterback. That position needed to be the calmest on the field; the one in control. Travis and control were two completely separate concepts right now.

The ball was snapped. Travis dropped back for a pass. He jumped left, then right, moving from opponents that weren't anywhere near him.

Travis was grandstanding. All the trained athletes in the bleachers knew it, but the announcer loved it. So did the cameras. People jumped to their feet waiting to see what he would do.

Two of his guys were open, but Travis didn't care. He tucked the ball into his chest, lowered his head, and plowed through the players. No one could touch him as he wove through the actors toward the goal line.

One actor reached for his flag as he approached the line. Travis smacked his hand away, twisting his body as he jumped for the end zone.

Travis never saw his brother in the path. As his body spiraled, his elbow went out, connecting with the back of Jake's unprotected head. Bone met skull and both brothers went down. Jake's head hit the ground.

Maya was on her feet along with a few hundred other people. If they'd been in regular football gear it would have been a minor accident. But flag football didn't require extra padding. Or helmets.

Nails and the medical team ran onto the field.

Jake wasn't getting up.

Chapter 19

No one would let Maya into the locker room.

It had nothing to do with the fact that she was a girl.

Nails had banned her from the area, according to the trainer who stood guard in the hall. The man didn't actually tell Maya she was banned, but he'd made it pretty clear that she, specifically, was not welcome inside while the doctor examined Jake.

On the bright side, Jake had walked off the field on his own power. No one carried him or brought out a stretcher. He didn't even lean on his dad for support. He just popped up, waved to the crowd, and walked to the sideline. Nails made him keep walking off the field.

Travis followed as well. The assistant coach took over for the Academy team, shuffled a few positions around, and restarted the game. Someone had decided to take a page out of the soccer team's playbook and instructed the guys to start playing it for laughs. The downside was that it looked like they were making fun of Travis now that he was no longer on the field.

It had been killing Maya that she had to sit in the stands to watch the last few minutes of the game. All she'd wanted to do was run out to check on Jake's physical health and Travis's mental health. But that would have sparked more photo opportunities and more stories for the Wall.

So she waited. She sat through every agonizing play. She stayed much longer than she should have, since she needed to get ready for her own match. That didn't matter. She had to find out what was happening.

When the final buzzer sounded and everyone jumped to their feet to cheer and try for a photo op with a celebrity, Maya made her move. She said good-bye to Renee and Diego, then ran for the locker room.

Then she waited some more.

The locker room door finally opened and Nails Reed came out into the hall. With a nod of his head, Nails dismissed the trainer who had been guarding the door.

"Maya, I thought you'd be at the tennis court by now," Nails said.

"I wanted to see how Jake was. And Travis."

"Jake is fine," Nails said, filling her with immense relief. "The medical staff is looking after him, but there doesn't appear to be a concussion. He was just a little dazed."

"That's good."

"Travis is another matter," Nails said. "I've never seen him play this poorly. I realize it was just an exhibition game, but he was erratic, unfocused. At first, I thought it was the press coverage. But he's been in the public eye since *US Weekly* paid us six figures for his baby pictures. No, the only new element in the mix is you, Maya. I thought teaming the two of you together would enhance my son's public image. I was wrong."

"But . . . but I didn't do anything!" Maya protested. "I stayed away from him all week."

"I appreciate that," Nails said. "But it doesn't matter. Image is about public perception. Travis has done a lot of damage to his image this afternoon. Whether you like it or not, you're tied to that image. This is going to impact both of you in a negative way."

"What if I care about my friends more than I care about my image?" Maya said.

"I'd say that makes you a very nice person," Nails replied. "But not a good businessperson. I have to look after my son's interests. I'm concerned with yours as well. I'm not saying that you can't be friends. I just want you both to think about your careers as much as your feelings."

Maya clenched her teeth. "I'll take that under advisement."

"Good," he said. "Now, I think you need to get to the tennis courts. I'm hearing something about Nicole King and a press conference that I don't like at all."

"Press conference? What press conference?"

"I don't know," Nails said. "Find out."

Nicole had already proven once in the past week that pairing her with cameras was a dangerous thing. Putting her together with the press before the big match that was the grand finale to the Expo? Maya didn't want to think of the ways this could blow up in her face. She also didn't want to think about how many different ways Nails could blame her for it.

Maya reached the courts just as Nicole stepped in front of the cameras. She wore an outfit from Esteban's line, another tennis dress that could be worn on the court or out on the town. At least it wasn't an ensemble from Maya's photo shoot.

Nicole had her wrist wrapped in a bandage the same shade of purple material as the dress. It matched perfectly, but it stood out like it was in bold colors with flashing lights.

She'd gathered the press together for the impromptu conference on the patio of Slice, placing herself in front of the sign for an energy drink the store had recently stocked. Maya suspected that an endorsement deal was probably in the works. Oddly, Jordan was nowhere to be found.

It was too late to stop what was about to happen. All Maya could do was watch.

Nicole flashed the crowd her highest wattage smiled. "Thanks for stopping by, everyone. I know you're all expecting the big matchup between me and Maya Hart, but I'm afraid that won't be happening today."

As shocked as Maya was to hear this, she couldn't help but be a little amused that Nicole didn't mention Primrose at all in her announcement. As far as Nicole was concerned, everybody had come to see her, not some pop singers who coincidentally had the most popular album in the country.

"It's time for me to come clean about my injury," Nicole said.

The cameras went crazy. This wasn't major world news,

but it was big to the gossip-hungry group that had collected for the Expo.

Nicole's smile faded. She looked down at the ground as if willing herself the strength to go on. Again, Maya was amazed by Nicole's acting chops.

After the appropriate moment had passed, Nicole looked up at her audience. "You've all heard the stories. I suspect one or two of you may have written a few of them as well." Another pause. She raised her wrist so everyone could get a good shot. The cameras went wild again.

"It's true," she continued. "I did injure myself in my match against Dona. My wrist has been in pain for the past few weeks. And I did finally consult a doctor. It's nothing major. And with a little bit of physical therapy, I should be ready for the Skyborne Cup next month."

Shouts rose from the gathered press. The loudest was: "Why did you hide it?" That came from several reporters.

"Stupid pride." Nicole almost looked embarrassed even though that was an emotion she probably never felt. "I didn't want it to look like I was making excuses. Dona played a great game. And she deserved her time in the spotlight again. I didn't want the story to become about how she'd only played so well because I was injured."

Maya was both impressed and disgusted. Nicole managed to come across as humble and noble at the same time.

"But my friend Maya Hart was right to out me," Nicole said to Maya's shock.

One camera swung around to find Maya, and others soon

followed. Great. Her image was going to be linked with Nicole's from now on as well.

"It's time for me to heal." Nicole's eyes locked on Maya through the crowd. "So that I'll be ready to kick my friend's butt if we happen to face each other in the Cup."

The raised voices in the locker room could easily be heard through the closed door. Maya couldn't make out what was being said, but she was fairly certain she knew who the speakers were. Nicole and Jordan were going at it. They weren't yelling, but the strained conversation was at a level of volume that a simple door could not contain.

It only took a brief second of debate before Maya said, "Screw it," and pushed the door open. The voices immediately fell silent. Both eyes turned to Maya as she strolled in.

"Hi," she said, as if she hadn't interrupted a thing. She dropped her tennis bag on the bench and pulled out her tennis gear.

"Oh, Maya," Nicole said. "I thought you were at the press conference. I had to cancel our match."

Maya laughed. Nicole knew very well she was at the press conference. "I was there. But the game isn't canceled just because you forfeit. We have a school full of students more than ready to replace you."

"Oh, I know." Nicole's smile broadened. "But, let's be honest, it's not going to be as big a draw if two nobodies play against Primrose."

"I actually agree," Maya said. "That's why I called in a favor."

The door clicked open behind Maya. She didn't have to turn to know who it was.

"Hi, Nicole!" Dona came in carrying a plastic bag full of clothes and equipment she and Maya had just bought at the pro shop. "So sorry to hear I hurt you when we played against each other. Maybe you need some extra practice before taking on more mature players."

Maya stifled a laugh. If this were a cartoon, steam would be coming off Nicole's head.

"Thank you for your concern," Nicole said through clenched teeth. "Jordan, we can talk later." Nicole left the locker room without uttering another word.

Maya, Dona, and Jordan watched her leave in silence themselves.

"Can I speak with you for a moment?" Jordan asked Maya once the door closed. "Privately?"

It didn't take a genius to figure out what Jordan wanted to talk about. Conveniently, Maya finally had an answer. She followed the agent to the far end of the locker room. She was about to thank Jordan for her interest, but she never got the chance.

"I'm assuming Nicole's latest stunt probably soured you on working with me," Jordan said.

"I didn't think for a second you were involved in that," Maya said. It was the truth. Jordan wouldn't risk her own reputation by letting Nicole host a press conference without her.

"Thank you," Jordan said. "But she is my cross to bear."

"You don't *have* to represent her," Maya said.

Jordan sighed. "Oh, Maya. I *want* to represent her. Once you strip away all the melodrama, there's a star in there. She's going to get bigger and bigger until she self-destructs."

Maya knew that it was true. All of it. "Can I ask you a question?"

"Of course."

"You let me drag this decision out for weeks," Maya said. "You got me a job pro bono. You even helped me keep the job when you didn't have to."

"There wasn't a question in that," Jordan said.

Maya tilted her head and raised her eyebrows. They both knew exactly the question she was asking.

"I like you, Maya," Jordan said. "You're going to be a star someday yourself. I'd be lucky to represent you."

"But it would drive Nicole insane."

"Absolutely."

"So . . . ?"

"Sometimes Nicole needs to be driven a little insane," Jordan said. "If only to teach her not to leave me out of the loop and not to fake injuries to milk media attention."

"You think . . ."

"Maya, it's my job to know my clients better than they know themselves," Jordan said. "If I don't see it, it isn't happening. Do you really think the one person to witness her having problems with her wrist was the last person she'd want to know about it?"

Just when Maya thought Nicole could no longer surprise her, she pulled another trick out of her tennis bag. Of course it made sense for Maya to see the injury. Once Nicole pushed her far enough, Maya would have to do something about it. And then no one would question whether the injury was real if Nicole had been forced to reveal it.

Jordan might think that the business world was not high school, but Nicole was going to do everything in her power to prove her wrong.

Chapter 20

Maya had never met a celebrity before coming to the Academy. Not unless she counted the guy who played the grapes in the Fruit of the Loom commercials, which she didn't. In the few months since she'd moved, she'd met a huge football star, two of her biggest tennis idols—with drastically different reactions—and the most famous guy in film. None of that compared to the pure star power she experienced the day of the Expo.

Of all the stellar talent she'd met since the opening ceremony, no one was bigger at the moment than Primrose. And no one had impressed Maya more than the sisters Vanessa and Miranda.

The twins had no egos, no entourages, and no attitude. But, better than all that, they could *play.* It was the first thing Maya learned when they introduced themselves. The sisters had been playing tennis for years. It was how they relaxed on tour and how they solved their arguments—also, often while on tour. Neither of the twins played at the level of Dona and Maya, but they managed to keep up fairly well.

They were on the third and final set. The day's finale didn't run as long as the other events of the Expo and it certainly wasn't anywhere near as long as Maya and Dona's match at the Open, but they still put on quite a show.

The four of them were all over the court, smashing the ball back and forth with impressive skill until Vanessa slammed a scorcher past her sister and the crowd exploded in cheers.

The twins pantomimed a fight across the court, but their smiles and laughter made it clear it was all for the crowd. Dona picked up on the act and pulled Miranda away from the net while Maya joined in, pretending to calm Vanessa. By the time they were done, they and the audience were laughing so hard, they had to take a short break. It was the most fun Maya had ever had on a court.

Once the game faces came back on, they took their positions on the court. They'd reached match point. Maya and Vanessa were in the lead. If they won this point, they'd win the game.

Even though it was Maya's turn to serve, she handed the ball to her teammate. Vanessa was the one most of the crowd had come to see. It was only fair that she get to give them the show they wanted.

Vanessa smiled and thanked Maya as she took the ball. Then she pounded a fierce serve over the net. Her sister returned it with an equal amount of force. The ball went back and forth between the four of them, crisscrossing the court until Maya and Dona got locked in a volley like the one that had peppered their match in the Toronto tournament.

The crowd faded away. Even her teammate disappeared as Maya focused on the ball and Dona. She fell briefly into a kind of tunnel vision where nothing else existed. When she came out of it, she was surprised to find herself alone on her side of the court.

The twins had slipped away, totally unnoticed by Maya and Dona. The singers cheered their teammates on, giving them permission to re-create their now famous match. Maya had been holding back. Dona, too, certainly. Now they both let loose.

Maya broke the volley with such force, she sent Dona running to catch the ball.

Dona smashed the ball back, sending Maya across the court.

It was freeing. Maya finally had the chance to just play again. No drama. No paparazzi. Just her racket, a ball, and a stellar opponent. This was why Maya had left her home to come to the Academy. Everything else was just noise. None of it compared to the music that came from the court around her.

Thump-pop.

Thump-pop.

Thump-pop.

Thump.

The ball hit the clay and whizzed past Dona.

The crowd erupted. Even Dona's teammate, Miranda, cheered.

Dona was the happiest of them all. She dropped her brand-new racket and raced to the net. Maya was already there to meet her in the middle.

"I want to see you do *that* when you take on Nicole King," Dona said, as if there was no doubt that match was in their future.

The twins ran out on the court, joining them in a group hug as so many cameras flashed around them, they lit up the courts in the fading sun. The stands quickly emptied as spectators filled the court to offer congratulations and get some pictures taken with the players.

After posing for more photos than she'd done in her life, Maya finally saw some familiar faces. Renee and Diego were coming toward them, holding hands. Cleo was right behind the couple, still rocking her new look. They exchanged hugs and congratulations.

"I never apologized for ruining your clothes, did I?" Cleo asked Maya.

"No," Maya said. "But it was for a good cause, so I'm okay with it. At least, until Grant Adams writes his . . . or *her* next article."

"That's not going to be a problem," Cleo assured her. "We came to an understanding. As long as he/she stops trashing me on his/her blog, I'll keep quiet about what I know."

"That seems like a fair agreement," Maya said. She was glad to know that one crisis had been averted. That cut back on the potential negative press coming out of the Expo, so Nails would be happy. There was really only one other possible story that could sour the event. Unfortunately, that one affected Maya as well.

After all the photos and the interviews and everything else, Maya was one of the last to leave the court. She'd agreed to meet Dona and the girls after she changed so they could hit the town. Maya could have gone off with them, but she'd hung back a bit, hopeful that someone else had been there. She got her wish as Travis pulled her into the equipment room.

"Are we having a secret rendezvous?" Maya asked. They were in an oversized closet, surrounded by tennis gear, extra nets, and other supplies for the court. It wasn't exactly a romantic spot.

"No," Travis said. "No more secrets. No more hiding our friendship."

"Travis, we're in a smelly, dark room where no one can see us," Maya pointed out.

"Well, yes, because today was horrible and there's a ton of press still on campus that I'd personally like to avoid," Travis said. "But tomorrow we can go back to being friends again."

"We haven't been doing so well at 'friends' lately."

"True," Travis agreed. "But that's what I need right now. Today was . . . It opened my eyes. This whole week did. I always thought Jake brought a lot of trouble on himself. Well, he does. But I think I understand it better now. Dad's hard on both of us. He's always been. I lived for his praise. Jake only heard the criticism. Eventually, we got to a point where I started getting all the praise and Jake got the criticism."

"Until this week."

"And that's the crazy part," Travis said. "I was criticized on television. I was made fun of on the field. But the thing that got to me the most was Dad. His big plan to deal with my appearance on *The Hype* was to keep me away from you. Maya, that show didn't focus on you and me. It was all about being his son. Being in his shadow. I have to make a name for myself."

"I agree," Maya said. "But I have to ask, what does that mean for us? Your dad doesn't want me around."

"It means we're friends again," Travis said. "Just friends."

"Nothing more?"

"Not right now," Travis said. "I want to be more. I do. But right now, I've got to get my house in order. I don't want to drag you into this."

"Travis, I'm already in it," Maya said. "That's what friendship is."

She wanted to tell him she was in it as friends or as something more. But he was right. It wasn't the time. Travis needed all the noise to calm down before he could focus on her. It was probably for the best, since Maya still wasn't sure what she ultimately needed.

Travis thanked her with one of their friendly hugs. Maya still felt there was something more to it, but she left it unsaid. It was enough to know he'd felt the same way. She could see it in his eyes as he let her go.

Travis peeked out the door to make sure the coast was clear. "You leave first. I'll follow after a minute."

"You really were serious about us being public friends starting tomorrow," Maya said.

“Not really. I just thought it would be fun to pretend like we’re spies or something having a clandestine meeting. We can’t take this stuff too seriously.”

Maya laughed. “Okay. But you go first. If any reporters catch me out there, you could be stuck in here forever.”

“Good thinking.” Travis put on his sunglasses, which were completely unnecessary since the sun had set. He pretended to raise the collar of an invisible jacket to hide his face as he slipped out of the equipment room.

Maya was laughing as he left. That quickly ended as she replayed their conversation over in her mind.

Travis was right. She needed to focus on her game, too. She didn’t come to the Academy for relationships. She came to be the best in her sport. Someday soon she’d go up against Nicole King and a bunch of other players as good as or even better than her rival. They might even have their match at the Skyborne Cup, which was a little over a month away. Maya was going to have to throw even more into her practices. There would be time for love later.

She pretended to put on her own pair of nonexistent sunglasses and hid behind her own invisible collar as she slipped out of the equipment room . . .

And walked right into Jake.

“What in the world are you two doing?” he asked with a bemused smile on his face.

“We were just . . .” There was no way Maya could explain it without sounding insane. “Never mind. What are you doing hovering outside the equipment room?”

"Waiting for you."

"Oh," Maya said. "How's your head?"

"Pretty good." Jake said. "I've got a hard skull."

"Tell me about it."

"Yeah," he said. "That's not the first time that joke's come up today. But, to beat the obvious clichés into the ground, that hit knocked some sense into me, too."

"Okay?"

"I've been doing this all wrong."

Maya was confused. "Doing what?"

"Trying to win you back," Jake said.

Now Maya felt like she was the one who suffered a head injury. She didn't have a clue what he was talking about. "What do you mean, 'trying to win me back?' You haven't been doing anything."

"Exactly," he said. "I wasn't doing all the stupid Jake things I did in the past. I stopped going out with other girls. I cut back on the partying. I threw everything into my game."

Maya had noticed that his game had improved. The rest of it was nice to hear, but it was news to her. "You kept leaving places as soon as I walked in the door. How was I supposed to notice if you weren't around?"

"I'm not saying the plan was perfect." Jake took her hands in his. "But I didn't totally disappear. Do you think I wanted to do some fashion ad campaign? To be that close to you when I knew you didn't want me around? And then you went running out on the shoot. It was obvious you would have preferred Travis to be your costar."

"Jake, I chose you over Travis first," Maya said. "Travis had nothing to do with us not working out. Not really. You did when you couldn't trust me for long enough to keep from falling into bed with Nicole."

"I get that now," Jake said. "I always thought Travis was better than me. Dad pit us against each other all our lives. Up until lately, Travis was just better at impulse control. Well, I'm getting better, too, Maya. I'm better at taking a minute to breathe. You know how I scared everyone because I didn't get up right away after Travis knocked me in the head? I wasn't unconscious. I was waiting. Because I knew if I got up right away, I'd take Travis right back down to the ground with me. Wouldn't that have made for a fun story on the Wall?"

"I'm glad you didn't," Maya said.

"Me, too," he said. "It was the first time I ever really stopped myself from doing what every part of me was screaming to do. And, yeah, I'm going to do stupid things from time to time. I'm going to mess up. But nobody's perfect. And someday, you're going to be able to move past how stupid I was with Nicole. You're just going to have to. Because, Maya, I *am* going to get you back."

Jake knew an exit line when he said one. He gave her that smile that ran through the Reed family, then he turned and walked away.

Maya couldn't help herself. She smiled as she watched him go.

Seth Sabal

MONICA SELES was awarded a full scholarship to a sports academy at the age of thirteen and attended a couple of sports academies during her career. She won the French Open at the age of sixteen and went on to become the number-one-ranked woman in tennis, winning a total of nine Grand Slam titles before retiring from the game in 2004. Monica was inducted into the Tennis Hall of Fame in 2009. She is now an ambassador for the Intergovernmental Institution for the use of Micro-algae Spirulina Against Malnutrition (IIMSAM) and a board member of the Laureus Sport for Good Foundation, using the power of sport as a tool for change. Her memoir, *Getting a Grip: On My Mind, My Body, My Self,* was a national bestseller.

PAUL RUDITIS has written licensed novels, companion guides, and graphic novels for a variety of television series ranging from *Charmed* to *The Walking Dead*. His original novels for teens include the DRAMA! series and the romantic comedy *Love, Hollywood Style*.